Your Baby Shall Leap Again

Your Baby Shall Leap Again

Sylvia Gardner

Litsa P. Ward
Editorial Midwife Publishing

Also by
Sylvia Gardner

Why Is My Hair So Curly?

Copyright © 2025 Sylvia Gardner

ORDERING INFORMATION

Quantity sales. Special discounts are available on quantity purchases by corporations, associations, and others, as well as orders by trade bookstores and wholesalers. Please get in touch with Mrs. Gardner at sylviagardner3395@gmail.com.

EDITORIAL SERVICES

Dr. Lita P. Ward, the Editorial Midwife
LPW Editing & Consulting Services
Editorial Midwife Publishing
lpwediting@gmail.com

COVER DESIGN

Danny L. Gardner, Jr.

ISBN: 979-8-218-65258-6
Published and Printed in the United States of America

DEDICATION

To my loving husband, Pastor Danny L. Gardner, Jr., thank you for covering me in prayer, encouraging me through every season, and believing in what God has placed within me. Your love is my anchor.

To my precious children— Naigel and Dantrell, you are my joy, my inspiration, and my reason to keep pressing. May you always leap boldly into the purpose God has designed for you.

To my beautiful mother, May Johnson—Your strength, wisdom, and prayers have carried me further than words can express. You taught me how to carry purpose with grace.

To my late grandmother, Mary Wooden— A true matriarch of faith. Your legacy lives in me. Thank you for showing me how to walk with God and stand with dignity.

To the ministries and movements birthed through obedience, The Queen Esther Program, Little Queen Esther's, I Am HER, Born to Blossom™, Mary's Pantry, and Salon of Excellence Incubator— Each of you represents a leap of faith, a divine assignment, and a harvest of surrendered yeses. May every person impacted continue to leap into destiny and walk boldly in their God-given identity.

To my spiritual daughters— Each of you carries something divine. I see the leap in your womb, and I pray this book ignites your next yes. You were born for such a time as this.

And to every woman who thought her womb was barren, God sent this book to remind you: You're still carrying something that will leap again. This is your sign. Your baby will leap again!

TABLE OF CONTENTS

INTRODUCTION
"THE SOUND OF MOVEMENT"

There comes a moment in every woman's life when she feels like the thing she once carried so confidently—has grown silent. The dream she nurtured. The vision she wrote. The ministry she birthed in prayer. The baby in her womb of purpose... has stopped moving.

You've tried to convince yourself it's just resting. Maybe it's just a quiet season. But deep down, you're afraid. *"What if it's gone? What if what I once felt kicking inside of me was just a moment, not a mandate?"*

This book was born for you. "Your Baby Shall Leap Again" is not just a collection of words—it's a prophetic declaration. It's a trumpet call to every woman who has felt forgotten, delayed, overlooked, or spiritually miscarried. It's a reminder that even when the womb feels empty, the promise is not dead—it's just waiting for a divine encounter. Just like Mary greeted Elizabeth and caused her baby to leap, this book is your Mary moment.

Through real stories, revelation, and raw truth, you'll journey through the silence, the pain, the pressure, and finally—the push. Each chapter is a heartbeat, and each page is a contraction moving you closer to your breakthrough. You'll cry, you'll confront your fears, but more importantly—you'll begin to feel something shift inside again.

Beloved, this is your season to leap. This is your time to give birth again. The movement you felt wasn't a mistake. It was a preview.

And now... your baby shall leap again!

"And it came to pass, that, when Elisabeth heard the salutation of Mary, the babe leaped in her womb; and Elisabeth was filled with the Holy Ghost." — Luke 1:41 (KJV)

Chapter One

When The Womb Feels Empty

There's a pain that doesn't bleed on the outside. It's the ache of carrying a dream no one else can see... a ministry that hasn't moved in months... a promise that feels overdue. It's that place where you once felt so full, so sure—that God was doing something big in your life. And now, suddenly, you feel empty.

I know that pain well. I know what it feels like to walk around smiling on the outside, but your spirit is groaning inside—like something's missing, something's wrong. You start questioning: *"God, did I miss You? Did I mess up? Is it too late?"*

It is a very real place of spiritual loneliness. This wilderness feels barren, where the winds of time seem to mock you, whispering doubts into your ears. Have you ever been there? I have. I've walked through this journey of emptiness, feeling like I was alone in my struggles. At the same time, everyone else around me seemed to be thriving.

There were seasons when I would look at other women— powerful women, polished women, purpose-filled women—and

I would want to be like them. But not because I didn't admire them. It was because, deep down, I felt like I wasn't good enough. I thought God had skipped over me. I thought maybe He hadn't called me to give birth to anything. I thought maybe I was just meant to clap for others while silently dying on the inside.

But that was a lie. And if you've been thinking the same thing, let me tell you—it's a lie for you, too. God doesn't just call the qualified. He qualifies the called. And since He doesn't make empty women, you were created to carry something sacred. Your womb may feel empty, but God is still working.

That baby inside you—the calling, the ministry, the vision—it's not dead. It's just resting. And sometimes God has to quiet the womb so He can stir the woman. Have you ever been in a season where it felt like you were just waiting? Waiting for the promise, waiting for the breakthrough, waiting for movement? There are times when all you hear is silence, but don't be fooled—the silence doesn't mean God is absent.

You see, Hannah cried bitterly before Samuel came. Sarah laughed in disbelief before Isaac was ever promised. And Elizabeth—bless her heart—she lived with the shame of barrenness for years... but the moment Mary entered her house, something leaped!

Empty doesn't mean barren. And silence doesn't mean forgotten. Sometimes, God allows us to sit in seasons of emptiness to prepare us for the fullness that's coming. Because if He gave it to us too soon, we wouldn't know what to do with it. If He opened the door before our character was ready, it would crush us. So He hides us, holds us, and sometimes... humbles us.

But don't mistake the hiddenness for punishment. No, this is preservation. This is preparation. And when you come out of it, you'll know it wasn't for nothing. Let me ask you something. What have you stopped believing for because it hasn't moved in a while? Was it the book? The business? The ministry? The restoration of your marriage or family?

Whatever it is, I came to tell you God didn't forget. Even if it feels like you're stuck in a season of stillness, there is life forming in the silence. You're not empty—you're incubating. And when the time is right, you're going to feel that baby leap again.

I remember when I was pregnant with my children, and one of the most exciting moments was feeling my baby move. That little kick, that flutter—it reminded me that something alive was growing inside me. But I also remember the times when I didn't feel movement. Those were scary moments.

Sometimes, I'd lie real still, waiting for that little nudge. Other times, I'd shake my belly a little—just enough to wake that baby up. And sure enough, I'd feel that tiny shift, that nudge, that gentle leap of life reminding me: *"I'm still here, Mama."*

And I believe that's what God is calling some of us to do right now—Shake your spiritual belly. You've been waiting quietly. You've been grieving silently. But now it's time to stir up the gift. It's time to rattle the womb and declare to your promise: *"You will not die in me; you shall live!"*

I don't know who this is for, but I feel the Lord saying that there are some dreams, some promises, and some ministries that have been lying dormant in you. And He is about to stir them up.

You are not stuck; you are in a state of incubation. God is preparing you for the moment when that promise leaps again. As a woman of God, you have the power to speak life into what's been silent. Your voice has authority, your prayers have power, and your declarations have an impact.

So I dare you right now, Woman of God—put your hand on your belly and prophesy to what's sleeping inside you. Declare to that dormant promise: *"You will not die. You shall live!"*

Shake your belly. Wake up the dream. Your baby shall leap again!

Testimony

I remember years ago when I was in one of my deepest seasons of waiting. I had just given up on the dream of writing a book. It felt like I was just spinning my wheels, pouring out into others but feeling empty myself. My heart would break every time I saw others living out their dreams, knowing that my promise felt so far away. But one night, as I was praying, I heard God clearly speak: *"It's not over. You will write. But I need you to stir up the gift in you."*

That night, I took the first step—I began to write. I didn't know how long it would take, how it would unfold, or even if I was good enough. But I trusted God. And step by step, chapter by chapter, my baby began to leap again. I believe He's calling some of you to take the first step right now. Stir up the gift in you. Your promise isn't dead.

Reflection Moment

"Lord, I've been quiet too long. But I believe something is still alive in me. Help me shake my spiritual womb and awaken every dream, promise, and calling You have planted. Let me feel the leap again. In Jesus' name, Amen!"

Journal Prompt

Take a quiet moment with God and write from the heart.

1. What areas of your life have felt spiritually empty or forgotten?_____

_____

_____

_____

_____

_____

_____

_____

_____

_____

_____

_____

_____

_____

_____

2. Is there something God once promised you that you've stopped believing for? _____

_____

_____

_____

_____

_____

_____

_____

_____

_____

_____

_____

_____

_____

_____

_____

_____

3. How do you plan to "shake your spiritual belly" and wake up what's been sleeping? _____

_____

_____

_____

_____

_____

_____

_____

_____

_____

_____

_____

_____

_____

_____

_____

_____

4. Write a letter to your baby (your dream, purpose, or promise), declaring that it shall live again. _____

_____

_____

_____

_____

_____

_____

_____

_____

_____

_____

_____

_____

_____

_____

_____

_____

Declarations Over Your Womb

Say these out loud with boldness and prophesy over your life:

- *I declare that my womb is not empty—it is full of divine purpose!*

- *I may feel still, but I am not stuck. I'm being shaped in the silence!*

- *I shake my spirit awake. Every dormant gift shall come alive again!*

- *My baby shall leap! My purpose shall rise!*

- *I am not forgotten. I am being prepared for something greater!*

- *God has not overlooked me. He has preserved me!*

- *I am carrying something holy, and I will give birth in due season!*

- *I believe again! I expect again! I'm ready to leap again!*

Chapter Two

Carrying a Baby No One Can See

To carry and love an individual in your belly for nine months, and not even know what they look like is something. Back in the day—before ultrasounds and gender reveal—you didn't know if you were carrying a boy or a girl. You didn't know what kind of personality they'd have. All you had was faith and a belly that kept stretching. The physical changes in your body were constant reminders that something was growing inside you. Still, it wasn't visible to anyone else. The world around you saw the bump but not the baby.

You hoped for the best. You prepared a space. You picked out names. But the truth was—you were carrying something invisible, something only God could fully see. And that's precisely what it feels like to carry a spiritual baby—a calling, a dream, a vision. It's moving inside of you. It's growing. But no one else can see it. And truth be told, sometimes you can't even tell what it is.

This is one of the most complex parts of spiritual pregnancy: the invisibility of it all and the feeling of being misunderstood. The frustration of feeling like you're carrying something precious, yet nobody else can recognize it, not even you sometimes.

I remember seasons where I would pray fervently, asking God, *"What am I carrying? What is it that You've placed in me?"*

The answers wouldn't come quickly, and sometimes, they wouldn't come at all. But even in the silence, I could feel something stirring inside, something deeper than just uncertainty or frustration. It was hope. It was anticipation. It was faith.

I've learned some invaluable principles in those seasons. When you don't know what you're carrying, you've got to lean in close to the One who does. The feeling of spiritual pregnancy can be agonizing. You see others around you giving birth to their dreams, their ministries, their visions—and it can feel like you're left behind. But here's the truth. Your timing is not their timing. Your journey is not their journey. God has a specific purpose for you, one that is uniquely tailored to your life, your calling, and your future.

God knows what's in you, even when you don't. He knows what He planted. He knows what's developing. And if you listen— really listen—He'll start whispering clues. He'll confirm it through a word, a Scripture, or a moment in worship. He'll start shaping your identity around what's inside, not what's visible.

Sometimes, those whispers come in the form of quiet assurances: a random Scripture that leaps off the page, a brief but powerful conversation with a trusted friend, or even a subtle, Spirit-filled nudge that tells you, *"You are not forgotten. You are still carrying something precious."*

When God plants a vision in us, it's often done in secret. He hides it for a time. Sometimes, it's for our protection. Other times, it's because the world isn't ready for what we're carrying. It's His timing, and His timing is always perfect.

But so many times, instead of leaning into Him, we go looking for other people to tell us what we're carrying. We chase titles. We seek affirmation and get frustrated when nobody sees what we see. And here's where the struggle lies: when you seek validation from people, you open yourself to the danger of disappointment. People won't always recognize what's inside you. They can't because they didn't plant it. Only God can see the fullness of what you carry, and He alone can speak the words of life over it.

This reminds me of the story of Mary and Elizabeth in the Bible. Mary, a young woman carrying the Savior of the world, visited her cousin Elizabeth, who was carrying John the Baptist. Both women were pregnant with promises that the world couldn't see, but when they met, Elizabeth's baby leaped within her. Elizabeth declared, "Blessed is she who has believed that the

Lord would fulfill His promises to her" (Luke 1:45). Sometimes, all we need is a moment of connection with someone who can affirm us, someone who knows what it's like to carry the unseen. That affirmation is powerful—it awakens us to the reality that we are carrying something sacred.

But here's the truth: no one else can fully explain what's inside of you... because no one else put it there. Only God can. He doesn't need a spiritual ultrasound to confirm what you carry. He's the Creator, the Designer, and the One who planted destiny in your womb before you ever knew your own name. He doesn't need a man's approval, and neither do you.

I have spent so many years frustrated, trying to prove my worth and my calling to others. It was exhausting. But as I began to understand this truth—that only God truly knows the depths of my purpose—something shifted inside of me. I stopped seeking approval from others. I stopped worrying about being seen and began focusing on being faithful in the unseen places. I began to walk by faith, knowing that what I carried was valuable and worth waiting for.

So if you've been feeling unseen... misunderstood... uncertain about what's really inside of you—breathe. You're not crazy. You're just pregnant with something divine. Let God be your guide in this season. Let Him name it. Let Him show you how to nurture it. Let Him teach you how to carry something unseen with grace, patience, and faith.

I think about the seasons of quiet. The seasons when no one saw the work I was doing behind closed doors. When I was learning, growing, and developing my spiritual strength, those were some of the hardest seasons but also the most precious. It was in those moments when I learned to trust that God was working in me even when I couldn't see the fruit.

God doesn't waste anything. He doesn't waste seasons of waiting, nor does He waste moments of silence. What may seem like a barren season is actually one of preparation. He is pruning, shaping, and getting us ready for the fulfillment of His promises. Because when the time comes, and that baby is born, the world will finally see what God knew all along: You were never empty; you were always expecting!

And just as the world will marvel at the beauty of what you carry, God will be glorified. He will receive the glory for every step of the journey, from the unseen conception to the final moment of birth. Every part of the process is part of His design.

Reflection Moment

Take a moment to reflect on the journey you are on. Think about the moments when you felt invisible, when you felt like no one saw the work you were doing, and when you felt the growth that was happening in the secret place. Now, consider how God is at work even in silence, preparing you for something incredible. Reflect on the lessons you've learned in the quiet and how they have shaped you into who you are today.

_____

_____

_____

_____

_____

_____

_____

_____

_____

_____

Journal Prompt

1. Have you ever felt unsure about what you're carrying spiritually? What made you question it? _____

_____

_____

_____

_____

_____

_____

_____

_____

_____

_____

_____

_____

_____

_____

_____

_____

2. What have others said about you that made you question your calling or purpose? How do you plan to take those thoughts captive and submit them to God's truth? _____

_____

_____

_____

_____

_____

_____

_____

_____

_____

_____

_____

_____

_____

_____

3. What is God whispering to you about the baby inside of you? How can you lean in more to listen for His voice?

_____

_____

_____

_____

_____

_____

_____

_____

_____

_____

_____

_____

_____

_____

_____

_____

4. Write a letter to God asking Him to reveal more of what you're carrying and how to steward it in this season. Ask Him to help you walk in the fullness of His purpose for your life. _____

_____

_____

_____

_____

_____

_____

_____

_____

_____

_____

_____

_____

Declarations Over Your Womb

- *I am carrying something holy, even when I can't see it clearly.*

- *I trust God to reveal what He has placed in me in His perfect timing!*

- *I release the need for external validation—only God knows what's inside.*

- *I am pregnant with purpose, and I will not abort my assignment!*

- *I will carry this baby full-term!*

- *I will walk by faith and not by sight!*

- *What God planted in me will be birthed for His glory.*

- *I may not see it yet, but I believe it's already growing.*

Chapter Three

I Carried It, But It Broke Me!

There's a unique kind of pain that comes from carrying something so precious, yet feeling like it's tearing you apart from the inside. I know what it feels like to carry something that God gave you—an assignment, a vision, a dream—and instead of bringing you joy, it brings tears, pressure, and crushing disappointment. You smiled on the outside while your belly of purpose was stretching you beyond what you thought you could endure. That pain was real, and no one saw it but you.

Sometimes, we don't discuss the emotional cost of carrying what God has placed within us. We assume it will be glamorous, glorious, and exciting. But the truth is—there were days I felt like I wouldn't survive the weight of what I was carrying. I often looked around at other women who seemed to have it all together, wondering why it felt so hard for me. Everyone else seemed to walk through their seasons with ease, their purpose carrying them with grace. But me? I felt like I was being crushed under the weight of my calling.

The truth is, it's often in those quiet, unseen moments of struggle that we experience the greatest transformation. When no one is looking, when no one is clapping or cheering, we find the true strength of God in our weakness. And though I didn't know it at the time, that's exactly where God needed me to be. He needed me to rely on Him more than I ever had before.

I remember nights when I cried myself to sleep, wondering, *"God, why would You give me this and not give me the strength to handle it?"* But the truth is, He did give me the strength—I just didn't recognize it in the breaking. Often, the breaking is the building. The crushing is the calling. The pain is the preparation.

I want you to think about the moments when you felt like the weight of what you were carrying would break you. Think about those moments when you couldn't see how you could go on. It could be a vision, a dream, or even a ministry that you felt called to. It could be your family, your business, or your marriage. What was it that you were carrying that was breaking you? The weight was heavy, but the truth is, it was preparing you for something great.

There is a breaking that doesn't mean death; it means birth is coming. We're so accustomed to thinking that when something breaks, it's over. But God uses brokenness to bring forth new life. He uses our tears, our pain, and our struggles to position us for what's next.

I've had those moments, too. I've had moments where I felt like everything I was working for was about to slip away. But just when I felt like giving up, I would hear God's whisper: *"It's not over. It's just the beginning."* And I would remember that pain is often a sign that something beautiful is about to be birthed.

I believe that pain is an indication that you're about to give birth. It's not always a sign that something's wrong— it's heaven's announcement that delivery is near. When I took Lamaze classes during pregnancy, they taught us breathing techniques. The purpose wasn't to eliminate the pain but to help us manage it, endure it, and push through it. That's what I believe God is doing in this season—He's teaching us how to breathe through spiritual labor.

The breathing techniques weren't just about controlling the pain. They were designed to help us focus and stay calm. In those moments, we had to trust that the pain wasn't the enemy—it was part of the process. When the pressure intensifies and the contractions of life hit harder, God's saying, *"Don't panic—breathe."* Because just like in the natural realm, when it's time to push, you can't fight the process. You have to lean into it and trust the One guiding the delivery.

Think about the contractions of life that you've faced. Those moments when everything felt like it was coming at you all at once—stress, pressure, uncertainty. It's easy to panic in those moments. It's easy to want to shut down and walk away. But what if, instead of running, we leaned into the pain? What if, instead of resisting the pressure, we trusted that it was all part of the process?

The enemy loves to make us believe that pain means failure. He loves to tell us that when things get hard, it's a sign that we're not doing it right. But in truth, pain is often the confirmation that we're doing it exactly how God intended. Just like a woman giving birth, pain precedes the arrival of something extraordinary. That pain is a sign that growth is happening and something new is being birthed into the world.

There are times when you'll feel like you can't go on, when you'll question your strength, your ability, and even God's calling on your life. But I want you to remember this truth: He will never call you to carry something without providing the strength you need to carry it. Even when you can't see it, He is strengthening you from the inside out. You are being refined in the fire, and that's a process that can't be rushed.

You may have carried your vision, ministry, business, or promise full term—yet it seems like the contractions of life are too much. But just like labor, it's the pushing through the pain that brings forth the miracle. There's always a moment when you feel like you can't take another step, but you push through anyway. You keep going even when everything inside of you is telling you to quit. And that's when the breakthrough happens.

I want you to know, Woman of God, you are not broken beyond repair—you are being shaped in the secret place. What you're feeling is not the end. It's the middle. And your baby will leap again. The pain that you feel is not the end—it's a sign that something powerful is being formed inside of you.

In this season, God is teaching us how to breathe through spiritual labor. We are learning how to endure, manage the pain, and trust God in the process. I know it's hard right now. I know it feels like you're being stretched beyond your limits. But trust me—when the time is right, when the baby is ready, you will see the fruit of your labor.

So, breathe, my sister! Trust the process. You are in the hands of the ultimate Creator, and He is faithful to see you through. The pain will not last forever. Your baby is coming, and it's going to be worth every contraction, every moment of uncertainty, and every tear.

Remember, the breaking doesn't mean it's over. It means you are being prepared for what's to come. Just as the pressure builds up before the birth of a child, your breakthrough is drawing closer. Keep breathing. Keep trusting. Keep pushing.

<u>Journal Prompt</u>

1. What pain have you experienced that might actually be a sign of your upcoming breakthrough? _____

_____

_____

_____

_____

_____

_____

_____

_____

_____

_____

_____

_____

_____

2. In what areas do you need to stop fighting and start breathing through the process? _____

_____

_____

_____

_____

_____

_____

_____

_____

_____

_____

_____

_____

_____

_____

_____

_____

_____

3. What does it mean to you to trust God as your spiritual "midwife"? _____

_____

_____

_____

_____

_____

_____

_____

_____

_____

_____

_____

_____

_____

_____

Reflection Moment

Take some time to reflect on the moments of pressure you've faced and how God has strengthened you through them. Write down the breakthroughs you are anticipating and the ways in which you are learning to breathe through the process. _____

_____

_____

_____

_____

_____

_____

_____

_____

_____

_____

_____

_____

_____

<u>Declaration Over Your Womb</u>

"I will not fear the contractions of life. The pain I feel is a sign that purpose is on the way. I breathe with the Spirit. I will not panic—I will push. I am graced for labor. My baby shall leap again!"

Chapter Four

I Had To Carry It Alone!

There are moments in life when you feel like you're walking a path of destiny, yet you realize that the journey you're on is one that you must walk alone. These are the moments when your calling becomes personal, and it's you and God—nobody else. It's in these solitary moments that we begin to understand the depth of our purpose and the true weight of the assignment we've been given.

It's not always a comfortable place to be. In fact, at times, it feels incredibly lonely. The people who you thought would be with you, the ones you imagined walking alongside you on this journey, may not be there. You may have felt abandoned, misunderstood, or even rejected. It's in these moments that you wonder why the path has to be so isolating.

When God calls you to a purpose, sometimes it requires a separation, a moment where you must carry your assignment alone. It's not that others don't care or that they aren't equipped to walk with you; it's that God has a deeper work to do inside of you in this season of solitude.

Some things can only be birthed when you're alone with God. There are depths that He wants to take you to that can't be shared with others until you've had your own personal encounter with Him. But it doesn't make it any easier.

I remember times when I felt like I was carrying the weight of the world on my shoulders. I was carrying visions, dreams, and responsibilities, and there were days when I felt like no one could understand. I'd cry out to God, asking why the journey had to feel so heavy. Why was I walking this path alone when I thought I would have more help, more support?

But what I've learned is that God often uses these lonely seasons to prepare us for the greatness He has in store. He's strengthening our resolve, deepening our faith, and refining our character. It's in the solitude that we learn who we truly are, what we're capable of, and how much we can endure when we lean on God for strength.

I think about the way a tree grows deep roots when it faces a storm. The winds may bend the branches, and the storms may come, but those roots grow deeper, anchoring the tree in a way that would not have been possible without the trials. Our seasons of solitude are like those storms. They may bend us, stretch us, and even break us, but in the end, we are stronger, more anchored, and more rooted in God's love.

There's something sacred about being in the wilderness with God. In isolation, He speaks in ways He can't when we're surrounded by distractions. It's there, in those moments of being alone, that He prepares us for the next season. He draws us closer, purifies our hearts, and sharpens our vision. It's often a time of preparation, a time when He's teaching us things that we wouldn't have learned had we not been alone.

In my own life, I've had to learn how to walk alone in many different seasons. Whether it was in my ministry, my marriage, or my calling, there were times when I felt the weight of everything I was carrying but couldn't seem to find the support I needed from others. I had to carry it alone. And while that's one of the hardest places to be, it's also one of the most transformative.

The thing is, God doesn't leave you alone during those times. Even when it feels like you're walking alone, He is right there, walking with you, strengthening you, and giving you the grace you need to keep going. But there's something about the solitude that brings you closer to Him, that helps you realize how much you genuinely need Him. It's like when you're in a crowd of people, but you're still feeling alone because no one truly understands what you're going through. In those moments, God becomes your Confidant, your Counselor, and your Comforter.

I had to learn to find my strength in Him, to realize that when I felt like I couldn't go on, He was there to lift me up. And that realization changed everything. It wasn't about waiting for others to help me or come alongside me; it was about trusting that God would provide everything I needed in those moments of solitude. It's not always easy to accept, but it's true: sometimes God will make you carry it alone because it's in the isolation that you discover the true power of His presence.

When I think about the journeys of great women of faith in the Bible, I think of Sarah, who had to wait alone for the promise of a child. I think of Hannah, who prayed for years without seeing the answer, but she carried that vision alone until the Lord opened her womb. I think of Mary, who was called to carry the Savior of the world. While she had support from Joseph, there was still a loneliness in the journey of carrying such a divine purpose.

Each of these women had to carry something extraordinary, and they did it in their own seasons of solitude. But in the end, their obedience brought forth miracles. And that's what I want to remind you of today: even when you have to carry it alone, the miracle will come. You may be walking a lonely road now, but keep walking. The breakthrough is coming!

You may feel like no one understands what you're going through, and you may even feel like you're the only one who's been called to carry the weight of this purpose. But in your season of solitude, God is refining you. He's preparing you for what's ahead. You may feel like you're walking alone, but you are never truly alone. The One who called you is walking with you every step of the way.

So, if you're in a season where you feel like you're carrying it alone, I encourage you to embrace it. Trust that God has a purpose for this season. He's doing a work inside of you that will prepare you for what's to come. Don't let the loneliness discourage you. Let it strengthen your resolve and draw you closer to the One who called you in the first place.

Remember, God never leaves you to carry the burden alone without equipping you with the strength to endure. He's with you. He's in the trenches with you, and He will bring you through. You are not alone. God is with you, and the best is yet to come.

Journal Prompt

1. Have you ever experienced a season where you felt like you had to carry your calling alone? What was that experience like for you? _____

_____

_____

_____

_____

_____

_____

_____

_____

_____

_____

_____

_____

_____

2. In what areas of your life do you feel lonely or isolated right now? How can you lean into God's presence during this time? _____

_____

_____

_____

_____

_____

_____

_____

_____

_____

_____

_____

_____

_____

_____

_____

3. What are the lessons God is teaching you in this season of solitude? _____

_____

_____

_____

_____

_____

_____

_____

_____

_____

_____

_____

_____

_____

_____

_____

Reflection Moment

Take time to reflect on the solitude you've faced in your life and how God has used those moments to draw you closer to Him. Write about the breakthroughs and lessons you've learned in your journey of carrying the vision alone. _____

_____

_____

_____

_____   _____

_____

_____

_____

_____

_____

_____

_____

_____

_____

_____

Declaration Over Your Womb

"I will not be discouraged by the loneliness of my journey. Even though I carry this purpose alone, I trust that God is with me. I will find strength in His presence, and He will equip me to carry this vision to fulfillment. I will not grow weary. I will keep going, knowing that the miracle is coming. My baby shall leap again!"

Chapter Five

When It Hurts To Carry

Carrying purpose isn't always beautiful—it can hurt. There are seasons when the weight of what you're carrying feels unbearable. It's not that you don't want to carry it, but it's heavy. And what's heavy can begin to hurt.

I've learned that pain isn't always a sign that something is wrong—it's often a sign that something is growing. When a woman's body begins to expand to make room for the life inside her, discomfort comes with it. Stretching doesn't feel good, but it's necessary for delivery. There's something inside of you that needs space, that needs to grow, and in order for that growth to happen, you have to endure the pain of expansion.

During pregnancy, we don't only stretch physically; our emotions stretch, our minds stretch, and our spirits stretch. And as much as we want to be prepared, we're never fully ready for how stretching will feel. The more you carry, the more it demands of you. There were times I found myself lying awake at night, questioning why something so beautiful had to hurt so much.

But in the stretching, I began to understand the divine process. I started to realize that my pain wasn't punishment—it was progress. It wasn't a sign that I was failing; it was a sign that I was moving toward fulfillment. The discomfort I felt was a part of the destiny I was walking into. The more I resisted the process, the longer the pain seemed to last. But when I leaned into the pain and accepted it as part of the journey, I began to feel a sense of peace.

I remember a specific night lying in bed, tears rolling down my face, not because I wasn't grateful for what God had placed in me, but because the process was wearing me down. I didn't feel strong enough to carry it. I felt isolated, misunderstood, and questioned by others who couldn't see what I was birthing. They saw me crying, but they didn't see the promise kicking. They didn't see the dreams stirring or the vision expanding inside of me, growing just beneath the surface.

The pain of carrying purpose is often misunderstood. People see your outward appearance, but they don't understand the inner workings—the quiet battles, the relentless prayers, and the sacrifices that come with being chosen. When you're carrying something of great significance, there will always be an aspect of it that others can't see that only you and God understand. And sometimes, it feels like you're walking through that process alone.

But I kept carrying it, even when it hurt. Even when I felt like I couldn't keep going, I took the next step. I reached out to God in prayer, asking Him for strength, endurance, and grace to make it through. And just as He always does, He answered. He strengthened my heart, my mind, and my spirit. The weight didn't feel as heavy because I started to realize that I wasn't carrying it alone. The weight was never intended to crush me—it was there to build me.

You may be in that very season right now. You're carrying something divine, something appointed, and it feels as if its weight is pressing you down. The pressure of purpose can sometimes feel suffocating, but if it's heavy, it's holy. God doesn't place weight where there is no value. He trusts you with this pregnancy of purpose. He has chosen you for this assignment because He knows you're equipped to carry it, even when it feels like the load is too much.

And yes, there will be moments when you question everything. There will be days when you wonder if you can really endure the pain. You'll want to throw in the towel and walk away from the very thing you once believed was your calling. But the truth is, you were made for this. You were made to carry the weight of purpose. You were chosen for this season because you have the strength to endure. And even when it hurts, you are still moving toward your breakthrough. You are still moving toward the miracle.

We often hear the phrase, "What doesn't kill you makes you stronger," but I've come to believe that it's more than just strength—it's about resilience. It's about learning to stand firm even when everything inside of you is screaming to give up. It's about learning to trust that God is using the pain to shape you for the purpose He has called you to.

If you're experiencing pain right now, I want you to know that it's not the end. It's just the beginning of something beautiful. There are women who have navigated immense pain in their lives—emotional, physical, and spiritual—and they have emerged on the other side stronger, wiser, and more equipped to fulfill their purpose. Pain is a part of the process, but it is not the final chapter. God is using the pain to refine you, to purify you, and to prepare you for what's coming next.

When you think about a diamond, it doesn't start out as a brilliant, sparkling stone. It starts out as rough, imperfect rock. But through pressure, heat, and time, that rock is transformed into something precious and valuable. The same is true for you. God is using the pressures of life to refine you, to shape you into the person He has called you to be.

There were days when the weight of purpose felt unbearable, but I pressed on because I knew that I wasn't just carrying a dream—I was carrying destiny. I wasn't just going through the motions of life; I was moving toward my purpose. I knew that every step I took, no matter how painful, was one step closer to the fulfillment of God's plan for my life.

When you're carrying purpose, there's a deep knowing that it's worth the struggle. It's worth the pain. The pain is temporary, but the promise is eternal. There may be days when you feel like you can't take another step, but I promise you that the strength you need is already within you. You were made for this. You were graced for this journey.

So, I want to encourage you today: keep carrying it, even when it hurts. When the pain is at its peak, remember that it's not a sign that you're failing—it's a sign that you're growing. The pressure you feel is making space for the greatness that is about to emerge in your life.

Keep carrying it, even when it's hard. Even when you can't see the end of the road. Even when it feels like no one understands. You are not alone. God is with you every step of the way. And in due season, your promise will leap again.

You are strong enough. You are capable enough. You are graced to carry.

Journal Prompt

1. What has been the most painful part of your journey of

    carrying purpose? _____

    _____

    _____

    _____

    _____

    _____

    _____

    _____

    _____

    _____

    _____

    _____

    _____

    _____

    _____

    _____

2. How has pain shaped your perspective or deepened your

   relationship with God? _____

   _____

   _____

   _____

   _____

   _____

   _____

   _____

   _____

   _____

   _____

   _____

   _____

   _____

   _____

   _____

   _____

3. What's one area where you need to give yourself more

grace as you carry? _____

_____

_____

_____

_____

_____

_____

_____

_____

_____

_____

_____

_____

_____

_____

_____

_____

Reflection Moment

Take a moment to reflect on your journey. Write down the painful moments you've experienced and how God has used those experiences to shape you. Think about how your pain has transformed into purpose and what lessons you've learned along the way. _____

_____

_____

_____

_____

_____

_____

_____

_____

_____

_____

_____

_____

_____

_____

Declaration Over Your Womb

"My womb is strong enough to carry the weight of my assignment. I will not fear the pain of purpose—I will embrace it, knowing that my discomfort is a sign of divine expansion. Even in the midst of hurt, I am still chosen, still appointed, still anointed. I am graced to carry, and I shall not abort the promise. I declare healing over my womb, strength in my spirit, and power in my push. In Jesus' name, Amen."

Chapter Six

Your Baby Is Still Alive

There were moments in my life when I honestly thought the dream inside of me had died. The silence was loud. I couldn't feel movement, and I couldn't hear God speaking. I couldn't see any signs that what He promised was still growing. I began to doubt if it would ever come to pass. The vision I once had for my life felt like a distant memory, a fleeting moment in time. But in those moments, I was reminded of something vital: ***Silence is not the same as death.***

There are also moments during pregnancy when the baby isn't moving, but that doesn't mean the baby isn't alive. Sometimes it's just resting. And spiritually, we go through those same seasons, where it feels like everything God said over us is asleep or silent. In fact, those seasons of quiet and stillness often precede something significant happening. God is working behind the scenes in ways we cannot see, and sometimes silence is God's way of preparing us for what's next. But I came to remind you that your baby is still alive.

When I was pregnant with my first child. I had gone past my due date and was ready to deliver, but something wasn't happening—I wasn't dilating. The doctors had to examine me, and they discovered that my pelvic bone was shaped differently. The baby's head couldn't come through. So, instead, I had to have a C-section. I was devastated at first, thinking, *"Why can't this happen the natural way?"*

And just like that, God gave me a revelation. Sometimes, the promise is too big to come through natural means, and the normal process won't work. God has to go in Himself and bring it out. And when He does that, it's because He knows you're carrying something special, something extraordinary that cannot be delivered through ordinary methods.

You've been wondering why it hasn't happened yet. You've been blaming yourself, wondering if something is wrong with you. But it's not you—it's the size of what you're carrying. The promise is so big, so different, so anointed, that it can't come the way everyone else's did. You might have looked around and seen others giving birth to their dreams, and you felt left behind or confused about why yours isn't coming to fruition in the same way. But I need you to understand something. It's not your fault!

And guess what? That's okay. Because the same God who formed the baby in your womb is the same God who knows exactly how to deliver it. God will not let what He has started in you die. He will not leave you abandoned in the process. You might not understand it right now, but He is orchestrating everything behind the scenes. Every step, every delay, and every moment of silence is part of His plan. Don't forget that His plan is better than our own.

What God placed in you is still breathing. It still has purpose. It still has power. And it's going to live. Even if you can't see it moving right now, I want you to know that there is life in what God has placed within you. The dreams, the vision, and the calling—none of it is dead. It's just waiting for the right moment to be revealed.

You just need to believe again. Speak life over it. Prophesy to your belly. Speak to the things you've given up on. Speak to those dormant dreams and say, "Live again!" Speak life into your business, into your ministry, into your family, and into the promises God made to you. Don't let the silence convince you that your promise has died. Just because you don't see movement doesn't mean nothing is happening. God is working behind the scenes, and He's about to bring it to pass in a way you never imagined.

I know it feels easier to give up when you don't see any immediate signs of growth. It's hard to keep going when it feels like you're not making any progress. But remember, the seasons of waiting and even the silence are often the times when God is preparing you for the bigger picture. It's like when a seed is planted in the soil. You don't see the seed growing beneath the surface, but it's working. It's rooting itself in the ground, gathering strength, and preparing to break through.

I want to encourage you to stay hopeful. Don't bury what's still alive. Don't let the silence fool you into thinking God has forgotten about you. He hasn't. He's simply allowing you to grow stronger. He's allowing you to prepare for what's coming.

When I felt that my dreams were dead, I started to declare over myself, "My baby is still alive." I began to remind myself of the promises God made to me. I spoke to my own spirit and reminded myself that God does not lie. His promises are yes and amen. If He said it, He will bring it to pass.

When God allows you to go through seasons of silence, it's an opportunity for you to dig deeper into Him and trust Him even when you can't see the outcome. The silence is an invitation to grow in faith, to deepen your trust, and to believe that even when you don't see things moving, God is still working. He's preparing you for what's to come.

You might be in a season right now where you're tempted to give up, but don't. Your baby is still alive. What God placed inside of you is still waiting to be birthed, and it's going to come forth in His perfect timing.

There were times when I felt discouraged and overwhelmed by the silence. I doubted that I would ever see the fruit of my labor. But as I look back now, I realize that every moment of waiting was building my faith. Every moment of silence was God preparing me to carry the weight of the promise when it finally arrived.

You have a dream inside of you that is still alive. You have a calling that is still active. Even if it feels dormant, it's not dead. God is still working, and He will bring it to fruition. Keep speaking life over it. Keep believing in it. Keep trusting that what God has placed in you will live.

I want you to speak these words over your life today: *"My baby is still alive. My dream is still alive. My purpose is still alive."*

Speak life, and watch the promises of God come alive in your life. Your baby is still alive!

Journal Prompt

1. What dream or calling did you assume was dead because you saw no movement? _____

_____

_____

_____

_____

_____

_____

_____

_____

_____

_____

_____

_____

_____

2. Have you ever confused silence with death? What is God

    teaching you in the stillness? _____

    _____

    _____

    _____

    _____

    _____

    _____

    _____

    _____

    _____

    _____

    _____

    _____

    _____

    _____

    _____

    _____

3. Can you recall a time God had to step in and "bring out" something because the usual way wasn't working?

_____

_____

_____

_____

_____

_____

_____

_____

_____

_____

_____

_____

_____

_____

_____

_____

Reflection Moment

Take time to reflect on the dreams you've let go of or forgotten about. Write down the things you once thought were impossible, and remind yourself that they are still alive. Ask God to reveal to you the areas where you need to trust Him more in the silence. _____

_____

_____

_____

_____

_____

_____

_____

_____

_____

_____

_____

_____

_____

Declaration Over Your Womb

"I declare that what God placed in me is still alive. I speak to my womb and command life to return to every dormant dream, every silent gift, and every delayed promise. My purpose shall live and not die. Even if it doesn't come the way I expected, it will come. I trust God to deliver what He promised. In Jesus' name, Amen."

Chapter Seven

The Moment of Leaping

In every woman's pregnancy, she experiences that very first flutter, that kick, or that jolt. That undeniable leap that reminds her—this thing is real. This life is real. Something is alive inside of me.

The moment of leaping isn't just about movement—it's confirmation. It's the awakening of the dream, the calling, the promise that was placed inside of you. In that moment, you can no longer deny the life that is growing within you. You realize that even though you couldn't see it before, something powerful was always there, just waiting for the right moment to spring to life.

It's that moment when everything aligns, and what was once silent suddenly makes noise. It's when what you've been carrying finally reminds you, *"I'm still here."*

This is what happened to Elizabeth in the book of Luke. The Bible says that when Mary greeted her, the baby inside Elizabeth leaped in her womb. And Elizabeth was filled with the Holy Ghost. That moment wasn't just a physical leap—it was a spiritual leap. A moment of confirmation that God was at work, that the promises of God were unfolding even in the quietest moments. And in the same way, your promise is stirring and moving within you.

Sometimes, all it takes is a word, a greeting, or a divine connection. Someone who is also carrying something great to show up, and suddenly your baby leaps. You've been waiting for a sign, and I came to tell you the moment of leaping is here.

It may not come with fireworks or an overwhelming rush of emotion, but it's still real. It may not be loud. It may just be a flutter at first. But make no mistake—it's leaping. You're not imagining it. Your dreams, your calling, your purpose—they're all coming alive. And while you may have felt like they were dormant, like they were lying in rest, the time of awakening is upon you.

I remember when I was pregnant, and there were times I didn't feel my baby move. I would get scared, worried that something was wrong. But most of the time, the baby was just asleep. And you know what I did? I would shake my stomach just a little— just enough to wake the baby up.

That's what this moment is. It's a divine shaking, a spiritual jolt. A reminder from heaven that what you are carrying isn't dead— it's just been resting. And now, it's time to wake it up.

The leap is here! It's not just about what you can see. It's about what God has already placed inside you, and now, it's stirring.

Now, it's moving. And you don't have to wait for it to look a certain way. Don't wait for it to come wrapped in the form you expected. The leap will come in its own unique timing, in its own unique way. You simply need to be ready for it.

This is your moment of leaping. Just like a baby inside a womb doesn't ask for permission to move, what God has placed inside you is not waiting for your permission to come forth. It's stirring and shifting, and the Holy Spirit is preparing you for the delivery of your purpose. It might be uncomfortable, it might catch you off guard, but it's moving, and that's a sign of life.

What you've been carrying isn't just a hope or a dream. It's a promise—a promise that you will see fulfillment. God doesn't give dreams to leave them unfulfilled. He's a promise keeper, and if He said it, He will bring it to pass. And just like that baby inside the womb that moves in its time, your dreams and calling will move in the fullness of time.

If you've been feeling disconnected from your purpose, discouraged by the delay, or uncertain about the future, I want to speak into your spirit right now! Your moment is coming. Your leap is coming. The time of waiting is over. You're about to see things come alive in ways you never imagined. It may not come in the grand way you envisioned, but even the smallest movement, the slightest flutter, is a sign that the promise is still on its way.

I recall a time when I thought my dreams were lost. I didn't see anything happening in the natural realm that gave me any indication that what God had promised me was still coming to pass. But then, there was a moment, the flutter, the small sign, when everything began to shift. It was a gentle reminder from God that He had not forgotten me.

That moment was my leap. It was a divine awakening. God was telling me, *"You are still pregnant with purpose. You are still carrying the promise I gave you."*

And I want to speak that over you today! You are still pregnant with purpose. Your promise is still alive, and your leap is about to happen. So don't fear the still moments. Don't be afraid of the silence. The quiet is just the time when God is doing His greatest work inside of you. The leap will come. It's just waiting for the right moment to manifest. And when it does, it will be undeniable. You'll feel it. You'll know that you know that you know—it's happening.

In fact, I challenge you today to begin to speak over your womb, over your dreams, over your calling. Begin to declare that the baby is leaping, that the purpose is awakening, and the promise is coming to life. Don't wait for the full delivery. Start rejoicing now, in the flutter, in the stirrings, in the small signs of movement. Those are signs of life, and they are signs of what's to come. The moment of leaping is here!

Journal Prompt

1. Who or what has caused something in you to leap recently? _____

_____

_____

_____

_____

_____

_____

_____

_____

_____

SYLVIA GARDNER - 72

2. When was the last time you felt spiritually "asleep"?
   What woke you up? _____

_____

_____

_____

_____

_____

_____

_____

_____

_____

_____

_____

_____

_____

_____

_____

_____

3. What does your leap look like in this season?

_____

_____

_____

_____

_____

_____

_____

_____

_____

_____

_____

_____

_____

_____

_____

_____

_____

_____

Reflection Moment

Take time to reflect on the dreams you've let go of or forgotten about. Write down the things you once thought were impossible, and remind yourself that they are still alive. Ask God to reveal to you the areas where you need to trust Him more in the silence. _____

_____

_____

_____

_____

_____

_____

_____

_____

_____

_____

_____

_____

_____

Declaration Over Your Womb

"I declare that the baby within me is leaping again. I will not fear the still moments because I trust the movement is coming. My womb is waking up. My purpose is leaping into alignment. I will not miss my moment. I embrace the kick, the jolt, the divine reminder that I am still called, still chosen, and still pregnant with promise. In Jesus' name, Amen."

Chapter Eight

Push Even If You Are Tired

There comes a moment in every labor where the exhaustion kicks in. Your body feels like it can't go any further. The contractions are stronger, the pressure is heavier, and the room feels like it's closing in. But even at that moment, when your strength feels depleted, the doctor will look you in the eye and say one thing..."Push!"

You don't push because it's comfortable—you push because it's necessary. In the spiritual realm, there are moments when your calling, your purpose, and God's promises begin to feel like a weight too heavy to carry. When the journey seems like too much, and your mind begins to question if the breakthrough will ever come, it's in these moments that God calls you to push. Even when the exhaustion is overwhelming, even when your body and spirit are spent, God says, "Push!"

Push not because it's easy. Push because it's necessary for your destiny. Your breakthrough is on the other side of that struggle, and every contraction, every moment of discomfort, is a sign that you are getting closer to what God has ordained for you.

There have been times in my life when I was spiritually, emotionally, and mentally exhausted. There were times I said, "God, I can't do this anymore." Times I cried and wanted to walk away. But then God whispered in my spirit, "Push, even if you're tired."

See, when you get close to birthing something great, the pressure increases. That's how you know you're near the promise. The intensity of the pressure and the weight of the task at hand are signs that God is preparing you for the new thing He is about to bring forth. It's not the time to give up, Sis—it's the time to press in. It's time to push through.

When I was in labor, I remember being so worn out from the pain and the waiting. I was past due. The baby wasn't coming. I felt defeated. But when they examined me, they realized I couldn't deliver naturally because of the shape of my pelvis. The baby's head couldn't pass through. So, they prepped me for a C-section.

That taught me something deep in my spirit. What you're carrying is too big to be birthed the "normal" way. Sometimes, the path to your destiny doesn't look like what you imagined it would. There are moments when the struggle seems too intense, and it feels like you're being forced down a path that wasn't part of your original plan. But don't worry—God has a plan. Even when you feel like it's too much for you, He knows exactly what He's doing. Quite often, God has to go in and bring it out Himself.

That doesn't mean the push was wasted—it just means He has a different delivery method. You still have to push through the fear. Push through the fatigue. Push through the disappointment. Because even when your strength is failing, His strength is made perfect in your weakness.

There will be times when it seems like you're on the brink of giving up. When everything inside of you says, "I can't go any further." But in those very moments, God is strengthening you in ways you don't even see. The exhaustion you feel is temporary, but the strength He imparts to you in those moments is eternal.

When my daughter-in-law was giving birth to her son. The doctor was preparing to give her a C-section. Still, he had another patient on the floor who was waiting for the anesthesiologist to come. I was in the room with her, and she was exhausted from pushing over and over again. The baby's head was almost out, but every time she stopped pushing, it would go back in. She felt like she couldn't do it any longer. Her energy was spent. But right when they mentioned the C-section, something rose up inside of her.

She found strength from somewhere deep within and gave one more push. That one push was all it took—my grandson came out! Sis, sometimes it takes giving all you have to bring forth what God has placed inside you. Sometimes you have to do it tired. Do it when you feel like you're at the end. Do it when they're talking about other options. Push, even if you're tired. Your baby is too close. Your promise is too near.

What you are birthing is just around the corner. The moment of your breakthrough is about to happen. And while the fatigue may be real, the delivery is even more real. God is faithful, and He will not let you fail. When you are faithful to push, even through the hardest of moments, God will give you the strength to bring forth the promise He has placed within you.

This is not just about physical endurance—it's about spiritual strength. It's about the strength you find in God when you feel at your weakest. His strength rises up within you. The Holy Spirit empowers you in the labor room of your destiny. When you push, you partner with God's will, and He equips you to complete the task.

You are not pushing in vain—you're pushing for purpose. You're pushing for the manifestation of your divine calling. You're pushing for the fulfillment of promises that have been spoken over your life. And just like the moment of delivery, your breakthrough will come when you least expect it, but at the exact right moment.

There's something profound about the process of labor and delivery. It doesn't matter how exhausted the mother is—the baby will come at the appointed time. The same is true in the spirit. Your purpose, your destiny, your dreams—no matter how long they've been delayed—will manifest when the time is right. But you have to push. And you have to push even when you're tired.

Don't stop now. You're too close to your promise to quit. Even if your strength is failing, remember that God's strength is sufficient. When you feel like you have nothing left to give, He will fill you up. He will give you the supernatural strength to push through to the other side.

Push, even if you're tired. The promise is on the way.

Journal Prompt

1. What in your life have you been tempted to give up on because of exhaustion? _____

_____

_____

_____

_____

_____

_____

_____

_____

_____

_____

_____

_____

_____

_____

_____

2. What do you believe God is asking you to "push" through right now? _____

_____

_____

_____

_____

_____

_____

_____

_____

_____

_____

_____

_____

_____

_____

_____

_____

_____

3. Write a letter to yourself reminding you why you can't

quit. _____

_____

_____

_____

_____

_____

_____

_____

_____

_____

_____

_____

_____

_____

_____

_____

_____

Reflection Moment

Write about the moments when you've wanted to give up and the way God has empowered you to keep going. What do you need to remind yourself of today to keep pushing? How can you tap into God's strength in your weakest moments? _____

_____

_____

_____

_____

_____

_____

_____

_____

_____

_____

_____

_____

Declaration Over Your Womb

"I declare that I have the strength to push. Even when I'm tired, even when I'm hurting, even when I feel unseen—I will push. I will not abort the promise. I will not forfeit my future. God is with me in the labor room of my destiny. I will deliver what He placed inside of me. My womb is aligned. My strength is rising. I will push, and I will prevail. In Jesus' name, Amen."

Chapter Nine

Prophets In The Womb

There is something sacred about carrying something that already has a voice before it's fully formed. The Bible tells us that before Jeremiah was formed in his mother's womb, God already knew him, consecrated him, and appointed him as a prophet to the nations. This truth is not just theological—it's deeply personal. It reveals that the womb is more than a physical space; it is a spiritual greenhouse where purpose germinates and prophetic destiny is cultivated.

What's inside of you is not random. It's not a fleeting thought or a vague hope. You are carrying prophetic potential—something God ordained long before the foundations of the world. It already has an identity, a name, and a voice. Even if others can't hear it yet, Heaven has already recognized and recorded it.

You're not just birthing a dream—you're birthing a divine message. You're not just pregnant with potential—you're pregnant with prophecy. That's why you often feel misunderstood. What's in your womb doesn't sound like the norm. It doesn't look like what others are doing. It doesn't follow the same timeline. But that's because it's prophetic.

Prophets are often out of step with the culture around them because they're tuned into a higher frequency. They speak to things that haven't manifested yet. They see beyond the present. They carry the future in seed form. And beloved, so do you.

The Spiritual Weight of Prophecy

There were seasons in my life when I couldn't explain the weight I felt. It wasn't depression. It wasn't anxiety. It was a divine heaviness—a pull to pray, a burden to weep, a stirring I couldn't shake. I would wake up in the middle of the night, heart pounding, with tears in my eyes and a yearning I couldn't explain. I thought something was wrong with me, but in time, I learned it was the prophet in my womb leaping.

It was the spiritual gift turning over, trying to find space to grow. It was the call of God stretching my soul to make room for destiny. If you've ever felt that kind of weight, that kind of holy unrest, then you know what I mean. That's not just emotionalism—it's divine movement.

You see, when you carry something prophetic, you're not just incubating an idea—you're hosting heaven's intention. And anything that carries heaven's DNA will bring warfare, misunderstanding, and pressure. But in the latter, it will also bring glory.

Misunderstood, but Not Misplaced

There are times you feel like an outsider, not because you're doing something wrong, but because you are carrying something right. People may question your choices, your pace, or your silence. They may mislabel your isolation as depression, your stillness as laziness, or your discernment as pride. But don't shrink. Don't apologize for the season you're in. You are in prophetic incubation.

Mary had to hide her pregnancy with Jesus for a season. She didn't announce it to the world. She didn't need public approval to validate her womb. She just obeyed. And in due time, what she carried changed the world.

You're not behind schedule. You're not being punished. You're being positioned. And when the time is right, what's in your womb will speak louder than any critic ever could.

Some Wombs Are Altars

Every woman doesn't just carry a baby. Some women carry blueprints. Some women carry mantles. Some women, like you, are pregnant with prophetic voices that will break generational curses, establish new bloodlines of faith, and declare the Word of the Lord in unprecedented ways.

Your womb is not just biological—it's spiritual. It is an altar. A consecrated place where God plants His intentions for the earth. And what an honor it is to carry something so holy.

This is why abortion of destiny is so tempting. The enemy knows he can't stop God, so he tries to wear you down until you stop yourself. He'll send discouragement, delay, and distraction. All to convince you that what's in you isn't worth the labor. But let me prophesy to you: ***YOU CAN'T ABORT THIS!***

Heaven is leaning over the balcony, waiting for your labor cry. Angels are assigned to help you push. The prophets in the womb are ready to speak. They are ready to shift cities, raise nations, and ignite revivals. But will you carry them to full term?

A Prophet's Cry Is Different

You may have wondered why your cry sounds different than others. Why do your tears seem to come from a deeper place? It's because prophets don't just cry—they groan. Romans 8 tells us that all creation is groaning, waiting for the sons and daughters of God to be revealed. That groan is prophetic. It's a sound of expectation, of urgency, of purpose.

When you groan in prayer, you're aligning with heaven's heartbeat. You're creating space for God's voice to be heard. That's what prophets do—they create space. They interrupt patterns. They confront comfort. They declare truth when lies seem louder.

You might not feel qualified. You might not have a seminary degree. But that doesn't disqualify your womb from being prophetic. God called Jeremiah before he ever preached a sermon. God appointed David before he ever wore a crown. And God has already chosen YOU!

Hidden But Marked

Some of the greatest prophets were hidden before they were revealed. Think of Moses. He was hidden in the reeds, raised in a palace, and called from a burning bush. Think of John the Baptist, who was hidden in the wilderness, eating locusts and honey, baptizing people in a river. Think of Jesus—hidden in Nazareth, a carpenter's son, unrecognized by many but divinely marked.

Being hidden doesn't mean you're forgotten. It means you're protected. God hides what He values. He allows obscurity to shield you from premature exposure. Let Him keep you hidden until the appointed time. What's in your womb will speak when heaven says it's time.

No Platform Needed

You don't need a platform to validate the prophetic gift in you. You don't need a stage or a microphone to prophesy. God has already declared your assignment before the world ever acknowledged it.

Just as Hannah promised God her son, Samuel, and followed through, we must dedicate what we carry back to the Lord. Samuel didn't just become a servant in the temple. He became the prophet who anointed kings, corrected nations, and heard the voice of God in purity.

That's what you're carrying—a mantle that has the power to anoint others. To speak life into barren places. To declare truth in dark corners. To heal what others have buried.

Your womb is not ordinary. Your gift is not random. And your voice is not an echo. You are an original sound.

Prepare the Room

It's time to prepare the room. Just as an expectant mother sets up the nursery before the baby arrives, so must you make room for what God has promised. Clear out the clutter of doubt. Sweep away the debris of fear. Open the windows of your heart and let expectation blow through again.

What you're carrying will need space. It will need discipline. It will need faith. But most of all—it will need your "YES."

Even if you're afraid, tired, or have failed before, say yes again. Carry it again. Believe again. Because the prophets in the womb are almost ready to speak.

Journal Prompt

Have you ever felt like what's inside of you was misunderstood or too "different" for others to grasp? Write about a time when you felt spiritually heavy or burdened—what do you think God was showing you then? _____

_____

_____

_____

_____

_____

_____

_____

_____

_____

_____

_____

_____

_____

Declaration Over Your Womb

"I decree and declare that my womb carries prophecy. I am not empty—I am full of purpose. What I carry will speak truth to power. The sound in my womb will be heard. I will not be silenced, delayed, or denied. Prophets are rising from within me, and they will declare the Word of the Lord without fear. I am a carrier of divine voices, and I shall bring them forth in God's timing."

"I speak to my womb and say: Awaken with purpose. Align with heaven. Expand with expectation. Birth what God has planted. I shall not miscarry. I shall not faint. I shall not doubt. I will carry the Word and deliver it in power. Amen!"

Chapter Ten

Leap Again, Woman of God!

There comes a moment when you've cried all you can cry, waited as long as you can wait, and questioned everything you thought you knew—and then, something leaps again. Something stirs. Something reminds you: You're still chosen. You're still called. You still carry promise.

The same womb that once felt empty now moves with expectation. The same belly that once felt forgotten now feels fire. And the same woman who once felt too broken to try again now hears God whisper, "Leap again, Woman of God."

You see, leaping is more than a physical reaction—it's a response to divine alignment. When Elizabeth heard Mary's voice, the baby inside of her leaped. Not because Mary was shouting but because purpose recognized purpose. When the right word hits your spirit, when destiny walks into your space, the baby in you must leap.

Some people will walk into your life and cause everything inside of you to come alive again. There are encounters, sermons, songs, and moments in prayer that wake up your womb and say, "This is your time."

You've been still long enough. You've played it safe long enough. You've questioned your call long enough. Now, it's time to leap again.

I speak to every broken place inside of you.

I speak to every delayed dream.

I speak to every hidden gift.

And I say, LEAP!

Leap like the woman of faith you are.

Leap like the overcomer you've become.

Leap with no fear, no shame, no apology.

Your womb is alive.

Your promise is real.

And the leap is your confirmation.

It doesn't matter how long it's been. It doesn't matter how many people counted you out. It doesn't even matter what didn't work last time. You're about to leap into your next.

So leap, Woman of God! Leap for the ministry. Leap for your healing. Leap for your calling. Leap for your family. Leap for yourself. And when you leap, don't look back.

<u>Why Do We Stop Leaping?</u>

Many of us stop leaping because disappointment becomes louder than destiny. We were excited once. We dreamed, we prayed, we prepared—but life hit us hard. Betrayal came. Finances dried up. The support system fell apart. And little by little, our faith muscles grew tired.

But remember this: the enemy doesn't attack what's empty—he attacks what's full. He saw the leap in you before you saw it yourself. He saw your potential, your impact, your ability to shift atmospheres, and so he whispered lies like:

- *"You missed your moment."*

- *"You're too old."*

- *"You're not anointed enough."*

- *"You'll never recover from that fall."*

But the devil is a liar! God is not finished with you yet.

Biblical Leapers: You're Not Alone

Let's look at some leapers in the Bible:

- David leaped when the Ark of the Covenant returned—
  because presence brings leaping.

- The lame man at the Gate called Beautiful leaped when
  Peter said, "Silver and gold have I none, but such as I
  have, give I thee..."—because healing brings leaping.

- John the Baptist leaped in Elizabeth's womb—because
  divine connection brings leaping.

- The woman with the issue of blood leaped in her spirit
  when she touched the hem of Jesus' garment because
  desperation and faith bring leaping.

So what about you? What's about to leap in you? Is it the book
you stopped writing? Is it the ministry you shelved? Is it the
prayer life you let grow quiet? Is it the courage to believe again?

Your Leap Will Wake Others Up

Do you realize that your leap isn't just for you? There's somebody else watching, waiting, and wondering if it's okay to leap, too. Your obedience to leap will spark boldness in others. Your testimony becomes someone else's permission slip to step into the deep. You're not just leaping for deliverance; you're leaping for legacy.

Think about Naomi and Ruth. One woman lost everything. Another woman followed her into the unknown. But through their connection and movement came the lineage of Jesus Christ. Imagine that—your leap may lead to someone else's redemption.

Leaping Past Pain

Leaping doesn't mean you won't limp sometimes. It doesn't mean you won't have flashbacks of failure or moments of weakness. But it means you've decided that what's ahead is worth more than what's behind.

Let's be honest. You may still have some scars. You may still be healing. But you're moving anyway. That's what makes your leap powerful.

The enemy wants you to wait until you feel "ready." But there is power in leaping while you're still bleeding, worshipping while you're still wounded, and trusting while you're still trembling.

You're Not Too Late

Time has not disqualified you. God operates outside of time. One divine moment can reverse 10 years of delay. When God says it's time, nothing and no one can stop it—not even you.

Sarah laughed when the angel said she'd conceive in old age. But her laughter turned into labor. What once seemed ridiculous became reality.

That's what happens when you leap. Heaven joins your motion. Doors open, windows break, and then favor flows.

Let This Be Your Leap Declaration

Let the devil know you're back.

Let fear know it doesn't have the final say.

Let doubt know you've recovered.

Let hell know you're not done.

Say it out loud:

"I'm leaping again, and this time,
I'm not shrinking back."

<u>Practical Steps for the Leap</u>

1. Pray Boldly – Not those "safe" prayers. Pray scary ones that stretch your faith.

2. Write the Vision Again – Pick up your journal. Write like it's already done.

3. Tell Somebody – Share your leap with a trusted friend. Accountability breathes consistency.

4. Sow into It – Faith without works is dead. Invest time, energy, and resources into your leap.

5. Speak to Your Womb Daily – Yes, prophesy over yourself every morning. Speak life to what's growing inside of you.

Journal Prompt

1. What would it look like if you fully leaped into your calling without fear? _____

_____

_____

_____

_____

_____

_____

_____

_____

_____

_____

_____

_____

_____

_____

_____

_____

2. What's been holding you back from fully trusting the baby inside of you again? _____

_____

_____

_____

_____

_____

_____

_____

_____

_____

_____

_____

_____

_____

_____

_____

_____

3. What are you afraid of losing by leaping? _____

_____

_____

_____

_____

_____

_____

_____

_____

_____

_____

_____

_____

_____

_____

4. Now, what could you gain? _____

_____

_____

_____

_____

_____

_____

_____

_____

_____

_____

_____

_____

_____

_____

_____

_____

_____

_____

_____

Declaration Over Your Womb

"I declare my womb is leaping again. I break every chain of stagnation, fear, and delay. I call forth my purpose, my gift, and my promise. I was made to carry greatness and deliver destiny. I leap with boldness. I leap with faith. I leap because God has ignited my womb once more. I shall not die with the baby inside of me—I will birth it, live it, and lead with it. Amen."

Chapter Eleven

Now, Walk In It!

Section I: The Moment After the Birth

There comes a holy hush in the room once the birthing is done. After the groaning, the pressing, the stretching, and the final push, silence. The moment the baby arrives, there is a sense of awe. Not just because something came forth but because you actually did it. You made it through. You survived the labor. What you carried in private now exists in public. It's no longer a dream; it's a manifestation. But here's the part they don't always talk about. What do you do after the baby is born?

For many women, both in the natural and the spiritual realms, there is a strange stillness after the promise comes forth. Not because there's nothing to do but because they're stunned by the shift. You prayed for this moment. You fasted for it. You cried for it. And now it's here. But your feet feel frozen. Your voice feels unfamiliar. You wonder, "Am I really ready to walk in this?" Let me be clear: Yes, you are.

You didn't survive all that pain to sit in spiritual silence. The contractions of purpose weren't meant to simply confirm your strength—they were meant to prepare you for movement. You didn't just birth a baby—you birthed a new you. And now it's time to walk.

The enemy loves the post-birth moment because he knows it's a critical window. If he can't stop the baby from coming, he'll try to stop the mother from rising. He'll whisper things like: You're not equipped. You're not ready. You're not the one. But let me tell you what God is whispering louder: "Daughter, arise. Now walk in it."

The time for waiting is over. The season of delay is done. Your womb has already confirmed you are chosen. Now, your feet must match your faith.

You've carried. You've labored. You've pushed. You've birthed.

Now, walk!

Section II: Prophetic Declaration — You Are No Longer Carrying; You Are Walking.

A divine shift must occur after birth. No longer are you just expecting—now, you are experiencing. The womb that once held the promise has released it into the world, and heaven is echoing: "Daughter, now walk in it." You're no longer in waiting mode. You're no longer nurturing what's hidden. What was once on the inside is now visible, tangible, and ready to be stewarded with boldness.

There's a transition in the Spirit that often goes unnoticed. After the miracle comes forth, many women linger at the altar of their past season—nursing their doubts, tending to fears, wondering if the next step is too big. But listen! You are no longer just a carrier—you are a walker, a doer, a builder. You were not made to stay in the delivery room. You were called to move forward with what came out of you.

Isaiah 30:21 declares, *"Whether you turn to the right or to the left, your ears will hear a voice behind you, saying, 'This is the way; walk in it.'"* This is not just a suggestion. It's an activation. A prophetic moment where heaven affirms that God is behind you, beside you, and going before you.

Walking in it doesn't mean you won't feel unsure—it means you move even when you are. It's easy to say "yes" to the promise, but now your feet must testify to that yes. This is your "go" season. No more rehearsing failure. No more bowing to fear. No more talking yourself out of what God has already approved.

Have you ever watched a newborn foal—wobbly and uncertain, trying to stand on its legs for the first time? That's you right now: a little shaky and wide-eyed. But you are walking nonetheless. Don't despise the awkwardness of your first steps. You don't have to look perfect when you walk—you just have to move. Heaven does not require you to perform; you simply need to be obedient.

The enemy will try to keep you in "carrying" mode long after the baby has leaped. He'll try to get you to nurture old assignments or return to the comfort of invisibility. But there's a holy call echoing through your spirit: *Daughter, it's time to walk!*

And not just walk aimlessly. Walk with authority. Walk with vision. Walk with grace. Walk like a woman who has been called, crushed, and commissioned.

You're not who you used to be. And you'll never fit back into the womb of small thinking. You've crossed over. Now, go forward.

Take the first step. Then, the second. And then keep stepping because the oil on your life wasn't given for you to sit still—it was given for you to walk it out.

Section III: Identity Activation

One of the greatest challenges women face after spiritual birthing is recognizing themselves. You've shifted. You've changed. You don't even cry the same, pray the same, or respond the same. That's not arrogance—it's transformation. The woman who entered the birthing room is not the same woman who is walking out of it.

So, the question is: Who are you now?

You are not just a survivor of the labor—you are the evidence of God's divine power to keep, to carry, and to crown. You are the result of crushing and pressing, of pruning and preparing. You've been reborn—not just into motherhood of the spiritual promise, but into the identity of a midwife, a mover, and a manifested woman of God. It's time to activate that identity.

Ephesians 2:10 declares, *"For we are God's handiwork, created in Christ Jesus to do good works, which God prepared in advance for us to do."*

Did you catch that? *Prepared in advance.* That means the version of you you're just meeting—God already knew her. He already wrote her path. He had already released grace for her assignment. All you have to do now is walk in it.

Let this be the moment you drop the labels others gave you before you gave birth. They called you emotional, unstable, inconsistent, or too broken. However, what they didn't see was the development process that takes place inside the womb. You were being formed into a woman of wisdom, war, and worship. And now that your baby is born, your identity must match the promise you made.

There's no room for impostor syndrome in this season. You are not faking it—you are becoming it. You are not stealing a lane— you are owning the one God paved just for you. This is your moment of identity alignment. It's time to speak it before you see it. Walk in who God says you are, even when your environment still echoes old names.

You are not "just trying something new." You are stepping into what has always been within you. You are not lost—you are located. The pain wasn't punishment; it was positioning. And now, you must walk like a woman who knows her identity is not a random discovery but a divine revelation.

Let's look at a few women who walked in what they carried:

- Deborah didn't shrink in the face of war—she rose as a Judge and Prophetess, walking in divine strategy.

- Esther didn't hide once she stepped into the palace—she used her access to birth deliverance for a nation.

- Mary Magdalene didn't stay in shame. After encountering Jesus, she walked in boldness to be the first witness of the resurrection.

And now you! You, too, are in that line of women who walked it out—even after fear, failure, or fatigue tried to stop them.

You've spent enough time doubting yourself. You've rehearsed the "what ifs" long enough. Now say this to your soul: *"I am her. I am the woman who was made for this. I am not going back into hiding. I walk in it, fully."*

This identity activation doesn't require applause. It requires agreement. Heaven is not asking for your perfection, just your yes. And once your yes meets your feet, the real journey begins.

So get dressed in your new identity. Put on strength like a garment. Clothe yourself in purpose. And start walking like a woman who knows who she is—even if she's still learning how to walk in it to become *HER*.

Section IV: The Cost of Walking

Walking in what you've birthed will cost you. This is the part we don't always preach. We shout over the birth. We dance over the vision. But walking? Truly walking in what God has called you to do? That will cost you relationships, comfort, the old version of yourself, and sometimes even your own desire to stay hidden.

The moment you decide to walk in your assignment, something shifts in the atmosphere—and not everyone around you will shift with it. Some will question your authority. Others will challenge your growth. Some will walk away because your elevation confronts their stagnation. But hear me clearly: you must keep walking anyway.

The cost of obedience is real, but the cost of disobedience is greater. Hebrews 12:1 tells us, *"Let us throw off everything that hinders and the sin that so easily entangles. And let us run with perseverance the race marked out for us."* Before you can run, you've got to release. You can't carry dead weight into your divine walk. And the truth is some things, people, some habits, some thought patterns—can't go where you're going.

Let's talk about a few specific costs:

1. *The Cost of Leaving the Familiar*

Familiarity doesn't always mean safe—it just means known. However, to walk in your promise, you must step out of your comfort zone. God called Abraham to leave his father's house and go "to a place I will show you." That's the cost: obeying even when you don't know where it's going to lead.

2. *The Cost of Misunderstanding*

When you start walking in power, people from your past will only remember your pain. When you step into purpose, some will accuse you of being prideful or "doing too much." But here's the truth: They don't have to understand your walk—they weren't in your womb, nor did they create what was on the inside of your womb. They didn't carry what you carried. They didn't labor how you labored. So they don't get to define how you walk.

3. *The Cost of Loneliness*

Let's be real—walking in obedience can feel isolating. You may find yourself walking alone in certain seasons. But you are never truly alone. God walks with you. He strengthens your feet, steadies your steps, and covers your path. He didn't just give you the baby—He's walking with you every step of the way.

4. *The Cost of Obedience Over Opinion*

Sometimes, the loudest voices aren't external—they're internal. It's your own thoughts that try to talk you out of your walk. *"What if I'm not ready?" "What if I fail?" "What if they laugh at me?"*

But, daughter, your obedience matters more than anyone's opinion, including your own. God didn't ask for your resume—He asked for your yes.

You will have to sacrifice comfort for calling, silence for speaking, hiding for healing, sitting for stepping. It will be uncomfortable at times, but it will be worth it. Because walking in it is not about how you feel; it's about what God said.

Yes, it will cost you. But remember—what you gain will far outweigh what you lose. You're walking into destiny. You're walking into legacy. You're walking into impact. This is the path where God gets the glory, and you get the victory, not just for you but for everyone connected to you.

So don't shrink because it's costly. Don't settle because it's lonely. Don't silence yourself because no one understands. Walk anyway.

Section V: Daily Walking with God

Walking in your purpose isn't a one-time event—it's a daily decision. Every single day, you have to wake up and choose to walk in it. Some days, your steps will be bold and confident. On other days, they'll be shaky and unsure. But what matters most is consistency. You may not always feel strong, but if you stay connected to the One who gave you the baby, you will be sustained.

Walking with God means allowing Him to guide your every move. It means pausing when He says 'pause' and moving when He says 'go.' It's not about your pace—it's about your posture. The Lord doesn't expect you to run before you're ready, but He does expect you to walk with Him.

Micah 6:8 reminds us, *"What does the Lord require of you? To act justly and to love mercy and to walk humbly with your God."* God wants a walk, not a sprint. He wants communion, not performance. He's not asking you to be perfect. He's asking you to be present.

How Do You Walk Daily With God?

1. **Start with Surrender.**

   Every morning before your feet hit the floor, say this simple prayer: *"Lord, order my steps today. Don't let me walk ahead of You. Don't let me lag behind. Help me walk with You."* Surrender sets the tone for divine alignment.

2. **Stay in Step with the Spirit.**

   Galatians 5:25 says, "Since we live by the Spirit, let us keep in step with the Spirit." That means you can't afford to walk based on emotions, popularity, or trends. Your pace must be Spirit-led. What worked for others may not work for you—and that's okay. Your walk is unique.

3. **Talk as You Walk.**

   Walking with God is not silent. Talk to Him throughout your day. Invite Him into your decisions, your appointments, your meetings, your motherhood, your ministry, and your moments of weakness. Don't just visit God—walk with Him. Make Him your companion, not your emergency contact.

4. **Embrace the Slow Days.**

   Some days, your walk will feel slow. Progress will feel invisible. But remember, even slow steps are still steps. As long as you're walking with Him, you're still advancing. Don't despise the quiet seasons—they're where roots grow deep.

5. **Refuse to Walk Alone.**

   You're not called to isolation. Walking in purpose includes divine connections—people who encourage your walk, pray for your journey, and speak life when you feel stuck. Ask God to send those who can walk with you, not just watch you.

Daily Walking Builds Daily Wisdom

When you walk with God daily, you begin to see life from a different perspective. You don't react the same. You don't settle as quickly. You discern more deeply. That's the fruit of walking, not rushing. You'll hear God in the stillness. You'll notice how He moves. You'll begin to understand your own rhythms.

This is not just about carrying something for God—it's about moving with God. Walking in it means you walk in step with heaven's agenda for your life.

You'll have days where it's hard. You'll have moments where you wonder if you're truly called. But the beauty of walking with God is that He never lets go of your hand, even when your steps are unsure. Even when you stumble, He holds you up.

Psalm 37:23-24 says, *"The steps of a good man are ordered by the Lord, and He delights in his way. Though he fall, he shall not be utterly cast down: for the Lord upholdeth him with His hand."* That's your promise.

So walk every day with your head held high, knowing you're not alone. Heaven is with you. God is beside you. And the One who gave you the baby will give you the strength to walk with it daily.

Journal Prompt

Take a moment in stillness and reflect on the following:

1. Where am I hesitant to walk because of fear, doubt, or comparison? Write out the specific areas where you've felt paralyzed or unsure. Be honest with God—and yourself. _____

_____

_____

_____

_____

_____

_____

_____

_____

_____

_____

_____

_____

2. What has God already confirmed about my identity that I've been slow to walk in? Recall prophetic words, dreams, confirmations, or moments when you knew He was calling you forward. _____

_____

_____

_____

_____

_____

_____

_____

_____

_____

_____

_____

_____

_____

_____

_____

3. What does it look like for me to walk daily with God? Imagine a day fully surrendered to Him. What would change? What would stay the same? What small steps can you begin today? _____

_____

_____

_____

_____

_____

_____

_____

_____

_____

_____

_____

_____

_____

_____

4. Now, what could you gain? _____

_____

_____

_____

_____

_____

_____

_____

_____

_____

_____

_____

_____

_____

_____

_____

_____

_____

_____

_____

Declaration Over Your Womb

Lay your hand gently over your womb and speak this out loud:

"I decree that I shall walk in full alignment with the promises of God. I silence every voice of doubt, delay, and defeat. I walk boldly—not in my own strength, but in divine power. I will not shrink. I will not retreat. I walk in the confidence of a woman chosen, appointed, and anointed. My womb is not just a place of birth—it is a place of movement. Every vision I have carried shall grow legs and walk into destiny. I declare today I walk in it... Fully, Freely, and Fearlessly. In Jesus' name, Amen."

Chapter Twelve

The Birthing Room Is Now Empty!

Section I: The Silence After the Final Push

The birthing room was once full of movement—labor pains, midwives, prayers, and spiritual contractions. It echoed with travail, expectation, and the voice of promise. But now... It's quiet and still. Why? The baby has arrived! The push is over. And yet, there's an odd ache in the stillness.

Have you ever felt the silence that follows great spiritual labor? It's a strange space—not barren, but empty. Not hopeless, but hollow. You've birthed what God placed in you, but now the room that once held purpose and pain is eerily quiet. No more contractions. No more helpers. No more "You've got this, push!"—just a deep breath and a holy hush. And you wonder, *"What now?"*

This is the part we don't talk about enough—the emotional shift after spiritual delivery. The adrenaline fades. The voices are quiet. The crowd that gathered for your moment of birthing now disperses. And suddenly, you're left in the stillness... with the weight of what's been born and the echo of what's now behind you.

For every woman who's labored in prayer, pushed through the pain, and birthed the vision, there comes a moment when the birthing room empties and you have to adjust to the silence.

But hear this truth: the emptiness does not mean abandonment. The stillness does not mean God has left because the hush is holy. Sometimes, after the push, God clears the room so you can hear Him—clearly, intimately, uninterrupted. He removes the noise so you can tend to the newborn promise without distraction. The empty room is not punishment—it's preparation.

You are not alone. You are entrusted. And just because the midwives have exited doesn't mean God has. This space is not the end—it's the beginning of nurturing, growing, and maturing the very thing you carried in secret. The birthing room may be empty, but your arms are full. Full of destiny. Full of what once kicked in the dark. Full of what God has entrusted you to steward.

Don't let the silence scare you. Let it settle you. You're not waiting anymore—you're raising now.

Section II: What to Do After the Birth

After the baby is born—after the vision comes forth—what do you do?

This is the part where many women get stuck. We're prepared for the push. We pray through the labor. But when the birth happens, there's no manual for what comes next. The spotlight fades. The room clears out. And all you're left with is the weight of what you've been entrusted to carry.

Let me encourage you. After the birth comes the building. You've birthed the ministry, the book, the business, the breakthrough. Now, it's time to steward it. This part requires just as much faith as the labor did—but in a different way. You're not pressing through pain now—you're planting in peace. You're learning the rhythm of nurturing.

Naturally, a newborn baby doesn't thrive off labor—it thrives off nourishment. Likewise, your vision won't grow just because you gave birth—it will grow because you feed it, protect it, and invest in it.

Here's What to Do After the Birth:

1. Pause and Breathe.

The birthing process was intense. You need space to rest, reflect, and recover. It's okay to pause. Don't rush into performance. Take time to acknowledge the miracle of what's been born and how far God has brought you.

2. Begin the Bonding Process.

Just as a mother bonds with her baby through skin-to-skin contact, you need to bond with your purpose. Sit with it. Speak life over it. Get familiar with it. Know the sound, the smell, the feeling of what you've birthed. Don't let outside voices name your baby—you know what God gave you.

3. Create a Feeding Schedule.

Yes—spiritually and practically. How will you feed what you've birthed? Through prayer? Through studying? Through wise counsel? Through discipline? What systems are necessary to support the growth of this vision? Remember, starving the vision is just as dangerous as sabotaging it.

4. Keep Watch Over It.

New things are vulnerable. And the enemy would love to snatch it before it can mature. Be vigilant. Don't leave your vision unguarded. Cover it in prayer. Surround it with intercessors. Protect its atmosphere. Everything and everyone doesn't deserve access to your baby.

5. Accept the Shift.

You are not who you were before the birthing. And that's a good thing. You've changed. Your capacity has increased. Your sensitivity has sharpened. Your discernment has deepened. Let yourself grow into this next version of who God has called you to be. You're not just a dreamer now—you're a deliverer.

Post-birth seasons are often misunderstood. You may not feel the same fire, but that doesn't mean the flame is gone. You're just in a new phase—one that requires wisdom, care, and stewardship. Don't try to go back to who you were before the labor. That version of you no longer fits the assignment.

You've entered a new season. And while the birthing room may now be empty... your life is whole, full of promise, full of purpose, and full of opportunity to raise what you've been trusted with.

Section III: When It Feels Like Everyone Left The Room

The room was once filled with excitement, anticipation, and the energy of those who prayed, labored, and encouraged you through the process. But now, it feels as though everyone has left. The birth has happened. The spotlight is dimming. And you're left standing alone, wondering if anyone even noticed the miracle you just brought forth.

Has that ever happened to you? You've poured your heart into something and believed God for something big, and when it finally comes to fruition, it seems like no one is around to celebrate with you. The calls stop. The texts fade. The cheers turn into silence. You're left holding the very thing you gave birth to, but the audience has moved on to the next big thing.

This is one of the most vulnerable and often painful places to be—when it feels like everyone has left the room. When the birth is complete, it seems like no one is there to cheer you on. The emotions can be overwhelming. The doubts can creep in. The enemy will try to convince you that because no one is celebrating, it means your work isn't valuable or that your purpose wasn't important.

But hear this! Even if everyone leaves the room, you are never alone. God is still there. The birthing room may feel empty, but it is full of His presence. You may not see the applause of others, but you have the audience of heaven cheering you on.

When It Feels Like Everyone Left, Remember This...

1. *You Are Not Defined by Public Applause.*

It's easy to want the affirmation of people. We all want to be celebrated for our hard work and efforts. But God's favor does not require the applause of men. Your worth and calling are not determined by the crowd's reaction but by your obedience to God. Your purpose is still powerful, even in silence.

2. *God Is With You in the Empty Places.*

In the moments when it feels like no one is there, that's when God is most present. He is a Father who stays close to His children, especially when they are in transition. Even when the room is empty of human presence, His Spirit fills the void. He's always with you, even when no one else is.

3. *This Is a Season of Private Growth.*

While the world moves on to the next big thing, you are in a season where God is nurturing what has been born in the secret place. This is your time to deepen your relationship with Him, seek His guidance, and prepare for the next steps.

The absence of others does not diminish the value of what you've given birth to—it just means God is doing a private work, for now.

4. *There Is Beauty in the Quiet.*

Silence can be uncomfortable, but it can also be a place of peace, clarity, and reflection. Take this time to listen. Don't fill the quiet with distractions or noise. Let it be the fertile ground where you cultivate new ideas, pray for wisdom, and seek His next instructions.

5. *Your Baby is Not Dependent on the Applause of Others to Thrive.*

You've given birth to something that has eternal value. Whether the world recognizes it or not, your purpose is real. God's plans for you are bigger than the opinions of people. Your assignment doesn't end because others are no longer watching. It's still growing, it's still moving, and it's still going to fulfill its purpose, with or without an audience.

Be Encouraged in the Empty Room

In those moments of loneliness, when the room feels empty and the applause has faded, God is still at work. He is still developing you. He is still refining the vision. Don't be discouraged by the lack of external validation—take comfort in the fact that your labor was not in vain.

Remember, the most profound transformations often happen in the quietest seasons. When the room is empty, it serves as a reminder that God is preparing you for something even greater, something that will require maturity, focus, and profound trust in Him.

The audience may leave, but your assignment is permanent. The call on your life is still strong. And when the next season of celebration comes, you'll know that you didn't need anyone to affirm your purpose to believe in it. You walked in it by faith, and that's what truly matters.

Section IV: God is Still Writing The Story

It's easy to think that the story ends when the baby is born. The labor is complete, the vision is born, and now you're left holding the results. But in reality, this is just the beginning. The story isn't over. In fact, God is still writing it.

You've only seen the opening chapters of your journey, the ones filled with pain, hope, expectation, and the eventual release of your promise. But the middle of the story—the part where your promise begins to grow, mature, and take shape—that's the season you're walking into now.

Sometimes, after the initial excitement of birth, we can feel as though the story is over. The grand moment has passed, and now we're left with the day-to-day work of raising and nurturing what we've birthed. We begin to wonder if our story still matters, if it's still going anywhere, or if God is still moving in it.

Let me reassure you that God is still writing your story. The fact that the room is empty doesn't mean your vision is fading into obscurity. The silence is simply the space where God is orchestrating the next chapters. He's not finished with you yet, and He's certainly not finished with the work He's begun in you. The vision may be born, but the story of its fulfillment has just begun.

Here's Why You Can Trust That God Is Still Writing Your Story

1. *The Vision Isn't Just a One-Time Event.*

God doesn't work in one-hit wonders. The vision He gave you is not a fleeting moment; it's a long-term process. Just because the moment of birth has passed doesn't mean the vision is complete. The story unfolds as the vision evolves, transforms, and comes to full fruition. God is invested in the whole process, not just the birth. He is faithful in continuing what He started.

2. *Every Chapter Matters.*

In your story, there will be seasons of joy but also seasons of challenge and quiet. There will be moments of success but also moments of struggle. And each of those chapters is important.

Don't despise the "in-between" chapters—the ones that aren't as glamorous or celebrated. Those are the seasons that build character, refine your calling, and strengthen your faith. Trust that God is using every chapter to mold you into who He created you to be.

3. *God Works in the Quiet Spaces.*

While it may feel like God is silent now that the birthing is over, He's still working behind the scenes. In the quiet, He's doing a deep work in your heart and in the vision you've birthed. You may not see the immediate results of your labor but trust that God is orchestrating things you can't yet see. The story isn't over, and He's not done with you. He's still writing your victory.

4. *You Are a Co-Author in the Story.*

God has given you the responsibility to steward what you've birthed. You are not just a passive observer; you are an active participant in the unfolding of this story. You still have choices to make. You still have steps to take. You still have faith to live out. God has given you the pen, and He's trusting you to continue writing in alignment with His will.

5. *His Timing is Perfect.*

Just because the room is empty doesn't mean that your story is incomplete. It may be quiet right now, but God is orchestrating things in His perfect timing. You may not understand the delays or detours, but you can trust that His timing is always right. Even in the waiting, God is still at work.

<u>A Prayer to Seal This Moment</u>

"Lord, I thank You for the gift of this season. I thank You for the vision You've given me, the baby I've birthed, and the promises that are yet to come. I trust You with the silence in the room. I trust You with the story You are writing. Even when I can't see the next chapter, I trust that You are faithful. Help me to steward what I've birthed with wisdom, patience, and grace. I know that You are not finished with me, and I will continue walking in faith, believing that the best chapters are still to come. In Jesus' name, Amen."

Section V: Trusting the Process

One of the most challenging aspects of carrying and birthing a vision is trusting the process. From the early stages of conception to delivery, there are so many unknowns. You know what God has promised, but the path between the promise and the fulfillment is not always clear.

You may have received a word, a prophecy, or a vision of what's to come. You may have experienced the excitement of believing, praying, and even bringing your promise to life. But now, you're in the middle of it. You're holding the results, but they don't look or feel exactly as you imagined. You're in the quiet space, the "after" of the birth, and the fullness of what you envisioned hasn't yet manifested.

The question is, can you trust the process? Trusting the process means letting go of the need for control and allowing God to guide every step. It means embracing the uncertainties and the waiting, knowing that His plans for you are better than your own. Even when things don't unfold the way you thought they would, or when the progress seems slower than expected, you can rest assured that God is still in control.

Why Trusting the Process Is Essential

1. *Growth Happens in the Process.*

You've been called to walk out this journey because God wants to mature you. The process is the place where you are refined, strengthened, and equipped for the greater purpose ahead. Every trial, every delay, every moment of uncertainty is not wasted—it's shaping you. You cannot skip these stages if you want to be fully prepared for what God has in store. Embrace the discomfort, the pruning, and the lessons learned along the way. The process is just as necessary as the promise.

2. *Trusting the Process Means Letting Go of Timelines.*

One of the most challenging aspects of faith is timing. We often think that our vision should unfold according to our own schedule. We're eager for immediate results, but God's timing is perfect, even when it feels like it's taking too long. His timing is never late—it's always exactly when we need it. Trusting the process means releasing your grip on the clock and allowing God to work things out in His perfect way. Your vision will come to fruition exactly when it needs to, not a moment sooner or later.

3. *The Process Refines Your Faith.*

When we're in the middle of the process, it can be easy to get discouraged. We may question whether we heard God correctly or if the promise will ever come to pass. But these doubts are opportunities to strengthen our faith. God uses the waiting period to draw us closer to Him, to build our trust in His sovereignty, and to teach us patience. The process isn't meant to break you; it's meant to build you. It's in the waiting that your faith grows deeper, and you learn to lean into God in a way you never could have before.

4. *Trusting the Process Brings Peace.*

When we stop trying to control every detail and surrender our vision to God, peace enters. You can rest in knowing that God is still at work—even when you can't see it. Trusting the process frees you from the anxiety of wondering if you're doing enough or if you're on the right track. When you trust God's timing and His plan, you can find peace in the waiting. You don't have to have it all figured out. You just have to trust that He does.

5. *The End Result Will Be Greater Than You Can Imagine.*

If you've ever seen a seed grow into a tree, you know that the journey from seed to fruit takes time. The seed doesn't instantly become a full-grown tree—it goes through stages of growth, sometimes unseen but always moving forward. Your promise is like that seed. It's growing even when you can't see it. It's developing in the quiet spaces. And when it's time for it to manifest fully, you'll look at the end result and realize it was worth the wait.

A Prayer for Trusting the Process

"Lord, help me to trust the process. When I feel discouraged or uncertain, remind me that You are in control. I release my timelines, my expectations, and my need for control into Your hands. I trust that Your timing is perfect and that every step of this journey is part of Your plan. Even in the quiet and the waiting, I know that You are working behind the scenes, shaping me, growing me, and preparing me for what's to come. Give me the strength to continue, knowing that the promise You've given me will come to pass in Your perfect time. In Jesus' name, Amen."

Journal Prompt

Reflect on the vision you've carried and birthed. What does the "empty room" feel like for you right now? Is there a sense of quiet after the excitement, or do you feel unsure of what comes next? Write about the emotions and thoughts you are experiencing in this season. How can you embrace the process and trust that God is still at work, even when you can't see the full picture? _____

_____

_____

_____

_____

_____

_____

_____

_____

_____

_____

_____

Consider the lessons learned during the waiting and birthing process. How have you grown spiritually, emotionally, and mentally? What steps can you take in faith to continue moving forward, trusting that God is still writing your story?

_____

_____

_____

_____

_____

_____

_____

_____

_____

_____

_____

_____

_____

_____

_____

Declaration Over Your Womb

"I declare that even though the birthing room may seem empty, my vision is not over. God is still at work in me, and He is continuing to write my story. I trust the process, knowing that each chapter is leading me closer to the fulfillment of His promises. I release my expectations and timelines into God's hands, trusting His perfect timing. The silence is not a sign of abandonment; it is a space where God is refining, shaping, and preparing me for the next chapter of my life. I will walk in faith, knowing that the vision is alive and the best is yet to come. I declare that I am equipped for the journey, and I will not grow weary in the waiting. In Jesus' name, Amen."

Chapter Thirteen

She Believed, And So She Became!

Section I: The Power of Belief

There is a silent strength that rises when a woman finally chooses to believe—not just in a general sense, but deeply, unshakably, and personally. The moment she decides to believe what God says about her, something shifts. The heavens take notice. Hell gets nervous. And she begins to become what she was always meant to be.

The power of belief is the divine spark that separates the oppressed from the overcomer. It is the catalyst that moves you from carrying the potential to living a purposeful life. Belief births becoming.

The enemy's greatest warfare isn't always aimed at your circumstances—it's aimed at your belief system. If he can convince you to doubt, to shrink, or to settle, he can sabotage your becoming. But when a woman believes, really believes, she becomes unstoppable. Not because she's perfect but because she's persuaded. Persuaded that God can use her. Persuaded that His promises are true. Persuaded that her past isn't powerful enough to cancel her future.

Scripture tells us in Luke 1:45, *"Blessed is she who believed, for there shall be a performance of those things which were told her from the Lord."* Mary, the mother of Jesus, believed what the angel declared over her, even when it made no natural sense. She was a virgin, she was young, she was likely afraid—but belief made her womb available for the miraculous. Belief positioned her for destiny. And the same is true for you.

What Happens When You Believe?

1. *You Shift from Waiting to Becoming.*

Belief changes your posture. Instead of standing still and waiting for things to happen, you start becoming the woman who is prepared for what's coming. Belief activates movement. You begin to walk differently, speak differently, pray differently, and live with purpose. You're no longer wishing for change—you are becoming the change.

2. *You Silence the Voice of the Liar.*

The enemy is terrified of a woman who knows who she is. Belief silences the enemy's whispers that say, "You're not good enough," "You missed your chance," or "You'll never be her." Those lies begin to lose their grip when belief takes root in your soul. You start to identify with truth, not trauma, with your destiny, not your damage.

3. *You Prepare Your Womb for the Promise.*

The womb represents your spirit, your creativity, and your ability to carry something divine. When you believe, you make room for God to place something sacred inside of you. You no longer resist the weight of purpose—you welcome it. Belief opens the spiritual womb to receive, nurture, and deliver what Heaven has assigned to you.

4. *You Partner with Heaven.*

Faith-filled belief invites divine partnership. You're no longer trying to make things happen in your own strength. You're co-laboring with God. You believe that His hand is on your life and that He will finish what He started. This kind of belief brings peace in uncertainty, strength in storms, and hope in the waiting.

5. *You Begin to Emerge.*

You don't need to chase platforms, titles, or validation. When you believe, you begin to emerge into who you were born to be. The fruit begins to show. The oil begins to flow. Your life begins to reflect the glory of God, and others start to see the transformation in you, not because you announced it but because you have become it.

Section II: Breaking Agreement With Doubt

Before a woman can fully become, she must first break agreement with doubt. Doubt is more than just a fleeting thought—it's a subtle thief that partners with fear, insecurity, and trauma to sabotage your spiritual pregnancy. It's not always loud. Sometimes, it whispers in your ear when you're about to step into something new. Sometimes, it disguises itself as humility. Sometimes, it speaks through the voices of people you love. But in every form, doubt has one assignment: to delay your becoming.

Many of us didn't even realize that, at some point, we made silent agreements with doubt. Maybe it was when someone told you, "You're too much," and you decided to shrink. Perhaps it was when you failed, and you silently vowed never to try again. Maybe it was when you were rejected, overlooked, or misunderstood, and you began to think, *"Maybe I'm not really called to this."*

Doubt thrives in places where there is no confrontation. But today, Woman of God, we're confronting it!

What Does Agreement with Doubt Look Like?

- Saying, "I'm not ready," when God has already called you.

- Constantly needing confirmation, yet never moving forward.

- Downplaying your gifts or calling so that others aren't uncomfortable.

- Choosing comfort over obedience.

- Waiting for someone to "endorse" what Heaven already approved.

You cannot become what you are too afraid to believe. Breaking agreement with doubt is not just about silencing negative thoughts—it's about repenting for ever allowing them to speak louder than God's voice. It's choosing to reject every word that did not come from the mouth of God. It's saying, "I believe what He said about me, even when I don't feel it, even when others don't see it."

Doubt Keeps You Stuck—Belief Sets You Free

When Eve entertained the serpent in the garden, he didn't attack her with violence—he attacked her with doubt: "Did God really say...?" That one seed of doubt led to disobedience, which shifted the course of generations. That's the weight of what you carry when you allow doubt to remain unchecked.

You are carrying a legacy. You are carrying nations. Your agreement matters. But here's the good news: You can choose today to renounce doubt and come to an agreement with the truth. You can evict every lie you believe about your identity, your calling, your timing, your worthiness, and your future.

This is your moment to stand in the authority God has given you and declare:

> "I break every agreement with doubt, and I divorce fear. I reject the lie that I'm not enough. I cancel every cursed word spoken over my life. I come into agreement with Heaven's report, and I believe God. And, because I believe I will become!"

How to Break the Agreement With Doubt

1. *Identify the Root of the Doubt.*

Ask yourself: Where did this belief come from? Was it a painful experience? A parent? A failure? A comparison? Trace it to its source so you can uproot it.

2. *Replace It with God's Word.*

You can't just empty the doubt—you must replace it. Fill your spirit with scriptures that affirm your identity, your purpose, and your calling. Declare them daily. Saturate your womb with truth.

3. *Surround Yourself with Believers, Not Doubters.*

The people around you matter. You need voices that echo God's Word over your life, not ones that stir up insecurity or keep you playing small.

4. *Obey Even While Afraid.*

Courage isn't the absence of fear—it's obedience in the face of it. Sometimes, you'll have to move while your knees are trembling. That's okay. God honors your obedience more than your confidence.

Section III: Becoming Who God Always Knew You Were

Before you were ever formed in your mother's womb, God knew you. Not just knew of you—but intimately, deeply, and intentionally. He wrote every day of your life in His book. He designed you with purpose in mind, with glory in mind, with destiny etched into your DNA. You are not becoming someone new—you're becoming someone ancient in the spirit. You are becoming someone God already saw. Therefore, you are stepping into the version of you that already exists in heaven.

This becoming isn't about striving, performing, or proving. It's about returning—to the original version God had in mind before life tried to redefine you.

Who Did God Know?

- A woman who could carry both promise and pain.

- A woman who would war in prayer and still nurture her family.

- A woman who would rise from rejection and still walk in authority.

- A woman who would birth vision, ministry, business, and legacy.
- A woman who would break generational curses and speak life over her bloodline.

He saw you then. He sees you now. And He hasn't changed His mind.

Becoming Is a Return

Becoming is not always glamorous. Sometimes, it looks like peeling back the layers that trauma, rejection, and fear added to your identity. It seems to be about stripping away what people said you were and finding peace in who God says you are. It's not about becoming what the world applauds—it's about becoming who the King anointed.

This journey of becoming often happens in hidden places. Like David tending sheep. Like Ruth gleaning in fields. Like Esther being prepared behind palace walls. The world may not see you yet—but God is forming you in the secret place. But why, you may ask? Because what you're becoming is too powerful to be rushed.

God Is Not Surprised by You

There is nothing about you—your voice, your calling, your personality, your past—that surprises God. He factored it all in and still said, "Yes, I choose her." He looked at your scars and still saw strength. He looked at your story and still saw the significance.

Sometimes, we ask, "God, are You sure You want to use me?" And Heaven responds: "I never changed My mind."

The version of you that walks in boldness, authority, peace, and divine power is not far off. She is already inside of you. She is rising. And as you believe God, she will emerge.

Becoming Means Letting Go of Who You Were

To become who God always knew you were, you have to release who you thought you had to be. That version of you that performed for love. That masked version that tried to blend in.

That broken version that made agreements with pain just to survive. "She" is not required for the next season.

Becoming often feels like breaking. But it's not the breaking that destroys you—it's the breaking that births you. God is peeling away everything that's not you so that you can come forth.

A Divine Unveiling

As you continue to walk in belief, there will be a divine unveiling. It may not happen all at once. Sometimes, it's a slow unfurling—like a rose blossoming petal by petal. Eventually, the world will see what God has always seen. You will step into rooms that your old self couldn't survive. You will carry the oil that your former pain produced. You will speak with authority because your words are rooted in Heaven's truth.

You're not becoming by accident. You're becoming by divine appointment.

Section IV: Walking Boldly in The Becoming

Belief doesn't just cause you to become—it teaches you how to walk boldly in what you've become. The transformation is not complete when you simply acknowledge who you are in Christ. It's complete when you walk it out with boldness, grace, and divine confidence.

Becoming isn't a passive process. It takes intentionality. It requires you to show up as the woman you believe God has called you to be—even when you don't feel qualified, even when your knees are shaking, even when you have to lead while still healing. Becoming means moving forward with steps of faith, not just faith talk.

Boldness Is a Language

There's a sound to boldness. It's in your declarations. It's in your prayers. It's in how you speak to yourself in the mirror before you step into rooms that used to intimidate you. Boldness is not arrogance—it is Holy Ghost confidence that says, "I may not be everyone's choice, but I am God's."

Your boldness says:

- "I'm not shrinking to make others comfortable."

- "I will not dim my light because others fear its brightness."

- "I'm walking in what I was called to do—even if I have to walk alone."

Remember, David didn't wait for a title before walking boldly. He showed up on the battlefield with a slingshot and confidence in God. Esther didn't wait for the perfect moment—she went before the king, knowing her life was on the line. That's boldness birthed through belief.

Walking Boldly Requires These Three Things:

1. *Ownership*

You must own your calling. Own your testimony. Own your assignment. It's time to stop apologizing for being anointed. Stop downplaying what God has entrusted to you. When you walk in ownership, you don't need permission—you already have Heaven's approval.

2. *Obedience*

Boldness without obedience is just noise. True boldness is saying, "Yes, Lord," even when it doesn't make sense. It's trusting Him enough to step when you don't see the full staircase. Every obedient step is a bold declaration of trust.

3. *Endurance*

Walking boldly means you'll keep going—even when it gets hard. You'll keep believing when doors close. You'll keep showing up when the support is low. Because you know what's on your life is too precious to abandon. You've come too far to turn back now.

God Is Releasing Favor for the Bold

There is a unique favor reserved for those who walk boldly. It's the kind of favor that accelerates destiny. The kind that opens doors no man can shut. The kind that causes people to wonder, *"Who is she, and where did she come from?"*

That kind of favor flows to the woman who dares to show up fully as herself, wrapped in the oil of belief and clothed in the confidence of God's promises.

Boldness Is Contagious

When you walk boldly, you give others permission to do the same. There's a generation behind you—daughters, mentees, spiritual sisters—watching to see if you'll rise. When you walk in your becoming, you're not just fulfilling your assignment—you're activating others.

You are a blueprint and a walking testimony. You are a living reminder that God still calls women who are willing to believe.

Section V: She Believed, and So She Became

This journey—this sacred, sometimes painful, always purposeful journey—isn't just about birthing a promise. It's about becoming the woman who could carry it. The woman who once questioned her worth now knows she was chosen. The woman who once wrestled with identity now wears it like a crown. The woman who once doubted has declared, "Be it unto me according to Your Word."

She believed. Not just with her mouth but with her movements. Not just in prayer but in purpose. She believed when no one else did. She believed when the mirror didn't reflect it yet. She believed when the doors hadn't opened. She believed when the pain told her it would never happen. And because she believed, she became.

She became what others said she wouldn't.

She became what fear said she couldn't.

She became what she didn't even know was possible.

She became what Heaven always saw.

Belief Is a Key

Belief unlocked the womb. It released the leap. It made room for the prophet inside. Belief parted the Red Seas in her mind. It silenced the storms of insecurity. It broke the back of generational fear. Belief was the key—and she used it.

Belief is not just an act of faith—it's an act of war. When you believe in God, you declare war on every lie ever spoken over your life. You stand as a warrior, as a vessel, as a living temple of the Most High, and you say, "I choose to see me the way Heaven sees me."

She Is You

This isn't just about a woman in Scripture. It's not just about Elizabeth, Mary, Ruth, or Deborah. This chapter is your reflection. This *becoming*—it's happening in you. God is raising you up as a sign, as a witness, and as proof.

You are the miracle someone else is waiting to witness. You are the leaping someone else needs to feel. You are the midwife, and someone else needs to believe again. You are her!

And now that you've believed, you are becoming her more and more every day, with every yes, with every prayer, with every seed sown in obedience. With every step of boldness and every tear that watered your purpose, you are becoming her!

She Believed, She Became, And So Will You!

The same power that overshadowed Mary...

The same breath that formed Eve...

The same glory that rested on Deborah...

The same fire that ignited the upper room... lives in you!

It's your time to arise, Woman of God. You don't have to become her—you already are her. Now, walk it out. The world is waiting to meet the you that Heaven already knows.

Journal Prompt

"What lies have I believed about myself that hindered my becoming? And what truths from God's Word will I now choose to replace them with?" _____

_____

_____

_____

_____

_____

_____

_____

_____

_____

_____

_____

_____

_____

_____

_____

Write a letter to yourself from the perspective of your future self—after you've fully stepped into who you've become. Speak life, speak strength, speak faith. Remind yourself that this becoming was always destined. _____

_____

_____

_____

_____

_____

_____

_____

_____

_____

_____

_____

_____

_____

Declaration Over Your Womb

"My womb is aligned with the Word of God. I break every agreement with fear, doubt, and delay. I carry divine purpose, and I release it in due season. I believe what God has said about me, and because I believe, I shall become. I shall birth, build, and bless—nations are in my womb. I am becoming all that God predestined me to be. I decree that my belief has unlocked my becoming!"

Chapter Fourteen

Now, Walk In It! (Part II)

Section I: The Shift from Believing to Becoming to Walking

There comes a moment after you've prayed, cried, waited, labored, and believed—when God says, "Now walk in it." It's the moment when your faith is no longer just a feeling or a whisper in the dark. It's a command. A call to action. A shift from sitting in expectation to stepping into manifestation.

You've carried the promise.

You've labored through private pain.

You've survived the breaking.

Now—walk in the becoming.

Becoming is only the beginning. Walking in it is where you live.

Walking Requires Movement

To walk in something means you're no longer hoping for it—you're operating in it. Walking is active. It's consistent. It means you show up in alignment with what Heaven has spoken, even when your environment hasn't caught up yet.

We love the idea of becoming, but walking requires:

- Discipline: Staying in alignment with what you were called to do even when it's not convenient.

- Confidence: Not waiting for external validation before you step into internal conviction.

- Stewardship: Taking care of what God gave you—whether it's a platform, a business, a ministry, or a mantle.

Walking in it means, "I'm not waiting for a stage—I'll walk in purpose in my living room if I have to."

<u>Walking In It Starts in the Spirit</u>

Before you walk it out in the natural, you must walk it out in the spirit.

- See yourself healed.

- See yourself whole.

- See yourself speaking, building, and thriving.

- See yourself in alignment with God's Word.

If you can walk it in your spirit, you'll have the boldness to walk it in real life.

Section II: What It Looks Like to Walk In It (Even When You Feel Unqualified)

Let's be honest—stepping into your calling doesn't always feel like a grand entrance. It often feels like fear in your throat and fire in your bones. Or walking into rooms where you feel underdressed in confidence but overdressed in destiny and saying "yes" while your knees are trembling.

And yet, God still says, "Walk in it." Because He's not looking for perfection—He's looking for obedience.

God Qualifies the Called

One of the biggest lies the enemy whispers when you're about to walk in your calling is, "You're not ready."

But here's the truth. Readiness is not a feeling—it's a decision. And you don't have to be fully prepared to walk in something God already ordained.

Look at Moses—he stuttered. Look at Gideon—he doubted.

Look at Esther—she was afraid. Look at Mary—she was young and unmarried. Yet they walked in it. Not because they were qualified but because they were called. And when God calls you to walk in something, He also equips you with grace for the journey.

Walking In It Looks Like This:

- Speaking even when your voice shakes.

- Showing up even when you feel unseen.

- Leading while still healing.

- Trusting while still transitioning.

- Creating even when you're still being corrected.

It's the everyday faithfulness that says, "God, if You're with me, I'll keep stepping."

The Power Is in the First Step

The most powerful moment isn't when you arrive—it's when you begin. Because when you take that first faith step, Heaven responds. Doors begin to unlock. Favor begins to flow. Provision begins to chase you down. Why? Because you dared to move when you didn't feel ready.

That's what makes the walk holy. That's what makes it powerful. You're not walking in your own strength. You're walking in God's promise.

Section III: Walking With Authority—Not Just Identity

Knowing who you are is powerful—but it's not enough. You must also be aware of the authority you hold. Identity is the revelation. Authority is the demonstration.

God didn't just call you His daughter. He gave you the power to speak, bind, loose, shift atmospheres, decree, and birth nations. And too many women stop at knowing their name when God is calling them to walk in the *weight* of their name.

What Is Authority?

Authority is the legal right to act, speak, and move on behalf of Heaven. It's the divine backing that causes hell to tremble when you rise in purpose. It's the echo of "Let there be," still alive in your womb.

Authority is the oil on your life that can't be mimicked. It's the sound in your voice that demons recognize. It's the fire in your prayer that shakes rooms. It's knowing that "I'm not just walking—I'm ruling in the realm God assigned me."

Walking With Authority Looks Like...

- Speaking with boldness, even in small rooms.

- Praying with precision, not just passion.

- Binding what Heaven doesn't authorize.

- Commanding your day instead of reacting to it.

- Silencing the serpent with the Word, just like Jesus did.

Walking with authority is not arrogance. It's alignment. You don't have to shrink to make others comfortable. You were never meant to walk small. Your footsteps carry divine weight. Your presence is not optional—it's ordered.

Heaven Has Authorized You

Hell may try to accuse you, but Heaven has already affirmed you. You are Heaven's ambassador. You are a royal priesthood. You are God's mouthpiece in the earth. You are a carrier of Kingdom Solutions. And when you walk in that knowing, hell loses its grip.

Section IV: Don't Stop Walking—Even When the Road Is Long

There will be days when walking in it feels more like crawling through it. Days when the fire that once fueled you flickers under fatigue. When your "yes" feels heavier than your hope. And in those moments, you must remind yourself:

You didn't start this walk for applause—

You started it for the assignment.

Even Jesus Walked Weary

Jesus, the Son of God, walked with weariness. He walked through betrayal, misunderstanding, and grief. He even walked up Calvary's hill with a cross on His back—and still didn't stop.

So if the Savior had to walk tired, you're not less anointed when you feel the weight of it. You're human—but you're still chosen.

Endurance Is Part of the Call

The walk is not just about acceleration—it's about endurance.

- Can you keep walking when no one claps?

- Can you keep building when no one notices?

- Can you continue to obey when the oil costs more than expected?

Endurance is what separates those who start with hype from those who finish with Heaven's help. However, walking in it will demand:

- A pace of prayer

- A rhythm of rest

- A posture of perseverance

- A heart that remembers why you started

You're Not Walking Alone

And here's the good news... You're not walking by yourself!

- Angels are assigned to walk with you.

- The Holy Spirit walks in you.

- Jesus intercedes for you.

- Destiny walks ahead of you.

- Grace walks behind you.

So don't stop! Even if your steps are slow—keep stepping. Even if your eyes are full of tears—keep moving. There is glory on the other side of your endurance.

Section V: Walk Boldly; The World Needs What's in You!

You weren't called to hide. You weren't created to shrink back. You were made to stand tall and walk boldly because the world needs what's inside of you.

We spend so much time trying to qualify ourselves, but what we truly need is the boldness to walk into spaces and circumstances, knowing that God has placed something valuable, vital, and world-changing within us. The walk you are on is not just for you—it's for the generations waiting on the other side of your obedience.

Boldness Is Not the Absence of Fear

Boldness is not the absence of fear—it's the presence of faith in the midst of fear. Boldness is stepping forward even when your knees are knocking, and your heart is pounding because you know that God's call is greater than your concerns.

- Boldness says, "I may not have it all figured out, but I know that I am not walking alone."

- Boldness says, "I will speak up, even when my voice shakes."

- Boldness says, "I will serve, even when I don't see the results immediately."

- Boldness says, "I will start, even though the journey feels daunting."

The World Needs What's Inside of You

Imagine if Jesus had kept His voice silent. Imagine if He had never walked out in boldness to heal, teach, and love the broken. The world would have been forever altered. But He chose to walk boldly in the authority and mission placed on Him, and as a result, the world was changed forever.

Now, God is calling you to walk boldly into the spaces He's prepared for you. Whether it's a ministry, a business, or a family—you have been anointed for this moment. You have been assigned to this time. And the world is waiting for you to step into what God has called you to.

<u>The Impact of Your Walk</u>

Every step you take in obedience is a step that impacts:

- The atmosphere around you

- The generations to come

- The Kingdom of God advancing and...

- The lives that will be forever changed by your boldness.

The world doesn't just need your gift—it needs your faith, your courage, your obedience, and your boldness. The world needs your walk.

So, walk boldly, Woman of God! Walk with confidence. Walk with power. Walk with authority. Walk with grace. Walk knowing that as you step forward in obedience, the Kingdom moves forward with you.

Journal Prompt

1. Reflect on a moment when you hesitated to walk in something God had called you to. What was holding you back? _____

_____

_____

_____

_____

_____

_____

_____

_____

_____

_____

_____

_____

_____

_____

_____

2. How can you step out in boldness this week? Identify one area of your life where you feel God calling you to walk forward, even in fear. _____

_____

_____

_____

_____

_____

_____

_____

_____

_____

_____

_____

_____

_____

_____

_____

3. What are the key promises or Scriptures you can declare over your walk in faith, especially when things get tough?

_____

_____

_____

_____

_____

_____

_____

_____

_____

_____

_____

_____

_____

_____

_____

_____

Declaration Over Your Womb

"I declare that I am walking in the fullness of the purpose God has assigned to me. I will not shrink back or be intimidated by fear or insecurity. I am walking boldly into the destiny that is mine. My steps are ordered by the Lord, and His grace empowers me to walk with authority and confidence. I will finish what I started, and I will see the manifestation of God's promises. In Jesus' name, Amen."

Chapter Fifteen

The Birthing Room Is Now Empty! (Part II)

Section I: The Birthing Is Complete—Now What?

The anticipation. The labor. The sweat. The tears. You've spent so much time carrying and nurturing the dream, the vision, the call—and now it's here. Your creation is in the world. What was once an idea has become a reality.

But now, there's a new feeling in the air. The birthing room is quiet. The weight you carried for so long is now lifted. But, now what?

The Moment of Release

The moment when the baby, the dream, or the purpose is finally released into the world is overwhelming. It's a moment of immense joy but also of profound silence. You've worked so hard to get to this point, and now it's out of your hands. What do you do when the labor is done, and there's nothing left but the quiet and the empty space?

The transition from carrying to releasing is often more difficult than the labor itself. When you're in the birthing process, everything is focused on the task at hand. But once the baby is born, you're left with the aftermath of that intense season, and sometimes, there's a feeling of "now what?"

You've crossed the finish line, but the work is far from over. You've released something into the world—but now you have to trust that the journey continues, even when it's no longer in your hands.

The Shift in Your Perspective

After giving birth, your perspective shifts. What was once inside you is now separate from you, and you must learn how to relate to it in a new way. Whether it's a ministry you've birthed, a business you've launched, or even a dream you've pursued, it now has a life of its own.

And just like a newborn, it requires nurturing, attention, and patience. But your role has changed. You can no longer "carry" it the same way. Now, you must watch it grow, even from a distance.

This is a sacred space. The labor is complete, but this is where the foundation is laid for growth. This is where you let go of your fears, your insecurities, and your doubts about whether it will succeed. It's time to trust the process and let go of control.

<u>Release Brings Freedom</u>

Although the transition from holding to releasing can feel disorienting, it offers a sense of freedom. The weight you carried has now been lifted, and though the journey may feel quiet and uncertain, it's also an opportunity for growth in new ways. It's an invitation to trust that the seed you've planted will take root and grow.

The release isn't just an end. It's a new beginning. You've birthed something that has the potential to touch lives, change hearts, and impact futures. And now that it's out in the world, you have to let it grow in its own time.

It's time to release the pressure, rest, and embrace the next phase of your journey.

Section II: The Emptiness Can Feel Lonely

The moment the labor ends, there's a sudden shift. The birthing room that once echoed with your cries of effort and anticipation now stands silent. The space that once felt full of movement and purpose feels oddly still. It's quiet. And in that quiet, the feeling of emptiness often follows.

The baby, the dream, the ministry—it's all out there now. But in this new season, you may find yourself wrestling with loneliness. You're no longer carrying something close to you, and the stillness can sometimes feel overwhelming. It's as if, after all the hard work, there's nothing left to do but wait.

The Silence Can Be Deafening

After all the action of the birthing process, the silence that follows can seem almost deafening. The world has received what you've birthed, but you may feel as if you're standing in a room where all the noise has disappeared. The crowds have moved on, the applause has quieted, and now, there's nothing but you and your thoughts.

In these moments, loneliness can begin to creep in. You might find yourself asking, "What now?" You've poured everything into this project, dream, or vision, and now that it's out there, you may feel disconnected from it. It's a painful yet necessary part of the process. But this feeling of emptiness doesn't mean that your purpose is over—it's simply a season of transition.

Loneliness in the Journey

You're not alone in feeling lonely after the birth of something significant. Even in the Bible, after the great works of God, there were moments of isolation and quiet. After leading the Israelites through the Red Sea, Moses found himself alone in the wilderness. Elijah, after defeating the prophets of Baal, fled to a cave, feeling abandoned and alone. But in those lonely spaces, God met them.

And just like Moses and Elijah, you're not alone either. It's in the quiet and the emptiness that God often speaks the loudest. When you can't hear the praise or see the results immediately, that's when you begin to hear His voice more clearly.

Recharging in the Silence

Though the emptiness may feel uncomfortable at first, it's important to remember that the silence is not abandonment— it's a sacred pause. It's in this pause that you have the opportunity to recharge, reflect, and realign your heart and mind for what's next.

Sometimes, in the busyness of birthing something new, we lose touch with ourselves. We often get so caught up in doing that we forget the importance of simply being. And in the emptiness, God provides an opportunity for renewal.

It's also a time to lean into what God has already done. The emptiness can be an invitation to be grateful for what has already been accomplished rather than focusing on what's yet to come. Take time to reflect on the beauty of what you've birthed and the impact it will have.

Learning to Trust the Process

When the birthing room is empty, you are not finished. This is simply a new chapter. You might feel lonely, but you are not alone. God's presence is with you even in the quiet spaces, and He is working behind the scenes. Your next steps will be guided by Him. Even when it feels like you're in a moment of waiting, God is still active and moving.

Trust that the emptiness will soon give way to new growth and new momentum. You are in a transition, but it's leading you to something greater.

Section III: Trusting That What Was Launched Will Thrive

Now that your creation is out in the world, it's easy to question what happens next. Will it grow? Will it thrive? Or will it fade away into nothing? As the birthing room empties and the labor pains are behind you, there's a space of uncertainty. But even in the quiet, God is at work.

The Work Continues, Even After Birth

Just because the work of labor is done doesn't mean the work of nurturing and growing is over. The baby you've birthed, whether it's a ministry, a business, or a vision, still needs attention and care. But this time, you have to trust the process.

In the early stages, it can feel like you're not seeing results. You put in the hard work and poured your heart into it, and now, all you see are small, humble beginnings. You might be tempted to doubt whether the seeds you've planted will ever grow.

But here's the truth: what is launched with purpose and faith cannot fail. Even if you can't see the growth immediately, it's happening. Like a seed planted in the soil, growth sometimes occurs beneath the surface. You can't always see the roots spreading, but that doesn't mean they're not growing. And in the same way, your work is growing, even when it feels like nothing is happening.

The Importance of Patience

Trusting that what you've launched will thrive requires patience. You cannot rush growth. You cannot force a seed to sprout the moment you plant it. It requires time, the right environment, and the right care. So, while you wait for the fruits of your labor to show, rest in the assurance that God's timing is perfect.

This is a season where you learn the value of patience. The Apostle James reminds us in James 5:7 that the farmer waits patiently for the valuable crop because he knows that in due season, it will come. And in the same way, your dreams and visions will bear fruit—just not always when you expect it.

God Is Nurturing What You've Launched

You are not alone in this process. God is nurturing the seeds you've planted, tending to what you've birthed with His perfect love and care. You may feel like you have to carry the burden alone, but remember, He is with you every step of the way. He's the one who orchestrated this journey from the start, and He is faithful to complete the work.

This is where your trust in God must deepen. You are called to trust Him not only in the labor but also in the release. You've done your part; now let Him do His. Your responsibility is to nurture and care for what's been birthed, but the growth—the ultimate thriving—belongs to God.

Declaring Life Over What You've Launched

While you wait for growth, there's power in speaking life over what you've birthed. Just because you can't see immediate results doesn't mean you should stop declaring success and life over it. Just as God spoke creation into existence, you, too, can speak life into your dreams.

Declare that your vision will thrive, that your ministry will flourish, and that your business will grow. Speak life, even when you can't see the evidence. There is power in your words, and by declaring life, you are inviting God's favor and increase to manifest in ways you can't yet see.

Trusting in God's Provision

When you trust God with the work you've birthed, you're also trusting Him with its provision. It may not always come in the way you expect, but rest assured, God will provide what is necessary for the success of what you've launched. Whether it's wisdom, resources, or divine connections, He will send everything you need at the right time.

Trusting in God's provision means learning to let go of your anxieties about the future and putting your faith in His perfect plan. What He has started, He will finish.

Section IV: Embracing the New Season

With the birth of your vision, dream, or ministry comes a new season. The moment you release what you've carried for so long, you step into a fresh chapter. It's easy to get caught up in what's left behind—the labor, the challenges, the waiting—but God is inviting you to embrace what is ahead. This new season is a season of growth, learning, and movement. But to fully step into it, you must embrace it with open arms, even if it feels unfamiliar.

The Birth of a New Season

When a woman gives birth, she doesn't just return to the way things were before. The birth of a child brings about an entirely new rhythm of life. Similarly, the birth of your dream, ministry, or vision will transform the way you live, think, and move forward. It changes everything.

Embracing this new season requires you to leave behind old mindsets, old fears, and even past disappointments. You cannot move forward with old baggage. God is calling you to shed the past and step confidently into what He has planned for you.

In this new season, God will take you through new experiences, new challenges, and new opportunities that will shape you in ways you can't yet understand. It's all part of His perfect plan.

The seeds you've planted are taking root, and what grows from this new season will be even more beautiful than you can imagine.

Adjusting to Change

One of the most challenging aspects of a new season is the adjustment. After birthing something, you may feel like you're stepping into unknown territory. The comfort of the familiar labor is gone, and the new season requires you to let go of what you once knew.

You'll likely face changes in your relationships, your schedule, and even your personal identity. It's normal to feel a little disoriented in the early stages. But it's important to remember that change is necessary for growth. Without change, there can be no transformation. You can't step into the fullness of what God has for you without embracing the newness He's bringing.

The beautiful thing about a new season is that it brings with it new possibilities. Opportunities that were previously unavailable to you will now come to light. What was once closed off is now open. You are stepping into a season where everything you've prayed for is coming to fruition, but it will require change on your part.

Trusting God in the Newness

As you embrace this new season, it's important to trust God. When everything feels new and unfamiliar, it's easy to second-guess yourself. You may even feel like you're not prepared for what's to come. But remember, God has prepared you for this moment.

The steps you've taken, the sacrifices you've made, and the work you've put in have all led you to this point. Don't doubt what you've already accomplished. God doesn't bring you to a new season without equipping you for it. He's already given you the strength and wisdom you need, and He'll continue to guide you through each step.

Walking in the Newness of Life

Embracing the new season also means walking boldly into the future. It's one thing to recognize that a new season is here, but it's another to actually step forward into it. You must be willing to walk by faith. Trust that God is guiding each step and that He will show you the way forward.

There may be times when you feel uncertain, and you might be tempted to go back to the familiar. But God is calling you to move forward, even if you don't have all the answers. Trust that He will reveal the path as you go.

In this season, don't be afraid to stretch, grow, and try new things. The birth of your vision was just the beginning. Now, it's time to live it out, to let it breathe, and to let it flourish.

Living with Expectation

As you embrace this new season, live with expectation. Expect that God will show up in powerful ways, that He will bring people into your life who will support and encourage you, and that He will continue to provide everything you need. The best is yet to come.

You've carried and birthed a vision with faith, and now you're stepping into a season where you will see the fruit of that labor. Embrace it. Celebrate it. Walk confidently in it. What you've worked so hard for is just beginning to grow, and there is so much more to come.

Section V: Moving Forward With Confidence

Now that the birthing process is complete and the labor pains are behind you, you are entering a phase where confidence is essential. As you step into this new season, it's important to hold your head high and move forward with the certainty that what you've birthed will not only survive but thrive. Confidence isn't based on what you can see at the moment but on what you know—God is with you, and He has equipped you for this journey.

The Foundation of Confidence

Confidence comes from knowing who you are in Christ and understanding that you are chosen for this moment. When God called you to carry and birth this vision, He didn't make a mistake. He trusted you with this task, knowing that you would be faithful to see it through. That trust should be the foundation of your confidence.

Psalm 139:14 says, "I will praise You because I am fearfully and wonderfully made." When you stand on the truth that you are fearfully and wonderfully made, you can face any obstacle with the confidence that you are equipped for success. God has uniquely prepared you for this journey.

Walking Boldly Into the Future

Confidence also comes from the willingness to walk boldly into the future. It's easy to hesitate, to second-guess yourself, or to wait for the perfect moment. But sometimes, the key to unlocking your success is simply to step out in faith.

God doesn't always give you a clear roadmap for the future. Sometimes, He asks you to trust Him enough to move forward, even when the path seems unclear. Confidence is the ability to step forward into the unknown with the assurance that God will lead you each step of the way.

Embrace this new season with boldness. God is calling you to take steps that may seem intimidating or risky. But with Him by your side, you are capable of overcoming any challenges that arise.

Faith and Action

Confidence doesn't just come from believing you can do it; it also requires action. Faith without works is dead (James 2:26). Moving forward with confidence means taking tangible steps toward your goals. It means stepping out of your comfort zone and trusting that God will guide your actions.

Take the steps He's leading you to take, even if they don't always make sense. Whether it's starting a new project, reaching out to a new audience, or taking a risk you've never taken before—take action, knowing that your steps are ordered by God.

Trusting God's Timing

While confidence involves action, it also requires patience and the understanding that God's timing is perfect. There will be moments when things feel like they're moving too slowly or when success doesn't come as quickly as you hoped. During these times, remind yourself that God's plans are always worth the wait. His timing is never too early or too late—it is always perfect.

You can confidently move forward because you trust that His plans for your life are greater than anything you could plan for yourself. He is working all things together for your good, even when you can't see how it will all unfold.

Celebrating the Journey

Confidence also involves celebrating the journey. It's easy to get caught up in where you're going and forget to celebrate how far you've come. The birth of your vision is a monumental accomplishment, and every step you've taken toward its growth is worth celebrating.

Take time to acknowledge the hard work, the sacrifices, and the moments when you wanted to give up but chose to keep going. Celebrate what God has done in and through you.

And as you celebrate, you'll find that the more you acknowledge His faithfulness, the more confidence you'll have to keep moving forward.

Releasing Fear and Doubt

Moving forward with confidence also requires releasing any lingering fear or doubt. Fear and doubt are natural, but they don't have to be controlling. They can't drive you in this new season.

When fear creeps in, remind yourself that you are not alone. God is with you, and He has not given you a spirit of fear, but of power, love, and a sound mind (2 Timothy 1:7). As you stand firm in the promises of God, you'll find that fear loses its grip and confidence becomes your foundation.

Walking in the Fulfillment of the Promise

The confidence to move forward comes from understanding that you're walking in the fulfillment of a promise. God doesn't call us to start something only to leave it unfinished. What He has begun, He will finish. So, walk in the assurance that you are walking in the fulfillment of His plan for your life.

As you move forward with confidence, keep your eyes on the goal, but don't be discouraged by setbacks or delays. Know that what God has launched in you is destined to thrive. Trust the process, and keep moving forward.

Section VI: Leaving a Legacy

After you've birthed the vision and begun to walk in it with confidence, there is one more layer that brings depth and meaning to everything you've endured: legacy. What you carry, labor with, and bring forth isn't just for you—it's for the generation behind you. The birthing room may now be empty, but what was birthed has the power to impact generations to come.

It Was Never Just About You

From the beginning, your pain had a purpose, and your process was part of a much larger picture. God entrusted you with something that would outlive you. The dream, ministry, or calling you've birthed will have ripple effects far beyond your current season.

A legacy isn't built in a single moment—it's established through obedience, sacrifice, and faithfulness over time. You may not always see the immediate fruit, but rest assured, what you've labored to bring forth is now on the earth to bless others, to set captives free, to heal broken hearts, and to shine light in dark places. You may never meet all the people who will be touched by your "baby," but they will walk in freedom because you said "yes."

Your Story Has Power

Your story—your journey through the birthing room—is now a testimony. Every contraction, every late night, every tear you shed, and every battle you fought is now a beacon of hope for someone else.

When people see you walking in what you've birthed, they'll know that the process was worth it. They'll draw strength from your testimony and courage from your transparency. Your story is not just yours—it's a roadmap for the next woman who wonders if she can make it through.

What you release into the world has eternal significance. It's not just about your name being remembered but about God's glory being revealed through your obedience.

Raising What You've Birthed

A legacy must be nurtured. Just like a mother cares for her child after birth, you must raise and steward what you've birthed. Protect it. Pour into it. Don't abandon it now that it's visible. The enemy would love to distract you into thinking your work is done. But what's been birthed must now be developed, taught, and matured.

Create systems around it. Build teams that believe in the vision. Speak life into it daily. God gave it to you because He knew you had the tenacity and grace to raise it well. Even in your tiredness, your obedience is still building a legacy.

Preparing the Next Generation

A true legacy is not what you do while you're here but what continues after you're gone. Begin to pour into others. Mentor, teach, and guide the next generation of visionaries. Share the wisdom you've gained in the birthing room.

Show them the scars but also the strength that lies beneath. Talk about the low moments, but don't forget to testify about the breakthroughs. Let your journey prepare them for their own.

Legacy means preparing others to pick up where you left off. You're not called to be the final chapter—you're just a powerful part of the story. Make room for those coming behind you to build upon what you started.

God Will Keep It Alive

If you ever worry about the weight of sustaining what you've birthed, know this: God will keep it alive. He's the one who gave you the seed, and He's faithful to water it and cause it to grow. Your job was to birth it; God's job is to sustain it.

Even when you're no longer actively involved, what you birthed will continue to move and bless others because God is breathing on it. His hand is on it. Your legacy is secure in Him.

You may have left the birthing room, but the baby—your dream, your purpose, your ministry—is alive, well, and destined for greatness. Keep building. Keep pouring. Keep leaving a mark that Heaven will honor.

Journal Prompt

1. Take a moment to reflect on what you have birthed in this season. What lessons did the birthing process teach you about yourself and about God? _____

_____

_____

_____

_____

_____

_____

_____

_____

_____

_____

_____

_____

_____

_____

2. How do you plan to steward what has been birthed?

_____

_____

_____

_____

_____

_____

_____

_____

_____

_____

_____

_____

_____

_____

_____

_____

3. In what ways are you preparing to leave a legacy for the next generation? _____

_____

_____

_____

_____

_____

_____

_____

_____

_____

_____

_____

_____

_____

_____

_____

4. Write a letter to your future self—or to a woman coming behind you—about what to expect when the birthing room is empty and the real work of legacy begins.

_____

_____

_____

_____

_____

_____

_____

_____

_____

_____

_____

_____

_____

_____

_____

_____

Declaration Over Your Womb

"My womb has served its divine purpose. I declare that what I have birthed will live, thrive, and fulfill its God-ordained destiny. I will not mourn the silence of the birthing room—I will rejoice in the sound of legacy moving forward. My spiritual womb is fruitful, my labor was not in vain, and my obedience has activated generational blessings. I shall walk with confidence, steward with grace, and lead with love. In Jesus' name, Amen."

Closing Declaration

"Sorry, Devil, But I Decided to Keep My Baby!"

"I have come too far to give up now. I've wept in the birthing room. I've bled in silence. I've warred in prayer. I've labored through seasons when no one understood the weight I was carrying. And now that the baby has been born, now that the vision has come forth, the enemy still dares to whisper, *"Give it up."*

But today, I make a public declaration to hell and all its forces! Sorry, devil—I decided to keep my baby. You thought I would miscarry under pressure. You thought the delays would break my spirit. You thought the loneliness would convince me to abort the promise. You thought if you attacked my body, confused my mind, or drained my strength, I would lay it down and walk away.

But you underestimated the God in me. You forgot that my womb was consecrated by the Word. You forgot that my contractions were a sign of coming glory. You forgot that my tears were watering a harvest that cannot be stopped. You forgot that I am not just a woman—I am a carrier of purpose, a protector of destiny, a midwife to generations. This baby, this ministry, this dream, and this mantle were never up for negotiation.

I will not give it up to fit in. I will not give it up to silence my voice. I will not give it up for comfort or convenience. I will not give it up just because others can't see the vision growing inside me.

I decided to keep my baby! I choose legacy over popularity. I choose purpose over pressure. I choose obedience over opinion.

I choose God's plan over my pain. So, to every demon that tried to convince me to abort, delay, or abandon—too late. I've carried it. I've birthed it. And now I'll raise it with fire in my eyes and victory in my voice. Because what I carry is holy. What I carry is necessary. What I carry is alive! And I will never apologize for choosing to keep what God put inside of me.

Sorry, devil, I decided to keep my baby!"

Conclusion: "The Baby Leaped, and So Did I!"

This journey wasn't just about a womb—it was about a woman. A woman who almost gave up. A woman who cried in secret. A woman who questioned if anything was still alive on the inside of her. A woman who felt empty, overlooked and forgotten by time. But God!

God whispered into her spirit, "What I put inside of you is still alive." And from that whisper came a leap. Not a physical one—but a divine stirring. A sign that what was dormant was only resting. A reminder that delay is not denial. And that every woman who carries a promise must also carry the faith to believe that it will leap again.

This book was never about a literal child. It was about the dream, the calling, the fire, the mantle, the ministry, and the purpose that was placed inside of you. You made it to the end. And you didn't just survive the pregnancy—you're standing in the victory of your birthing season. You fought through the silence. You pushed through the pain. You faced your fears and declared your faith. And now the world is about to see what you've been carrying all along.

So, hold your head up. Wipe your tears. Straighten your crown. Because this isn't the end. This is the beginning of a legacy. And if anyone asks how you made it, just smile and say, "My baby leaped, and so did I!"

Meet The Author

Sylvia S. Gardner

S ylvia S. Gardner is a dynamic spiritual leader, esteemed author, and passionate advocate for women and families. She serves as the Assistant Pastor of Greater Judah Christian Center in Winterville, North Carolina, where she co-pastors alongside her husband, Pastor D.L. Gardner. Married for 29 years, the couple has faithfully nurtured and led their congregation for nearly three decades, becoming trusted pillars in their community.

With a heart rooted in service, Sylvia Gardner has dedicated her life to empowering others—particularly women and young girls—to rise above adversity and embrace their God-given purpose. She is the Founder and CEO of Greater Judah Corporation, Inc., a 501(c)(3) nonprofit organization that addresses critical needs across eastern North Carolina. Under her leadership, the organization spearheads impactful initiatives such as *Mary's Pantry* and *The Little Queen Esther Program.*

Mary's Pantry, created in honor of her late grandmother, provides bi-weekly groceries to hundreds of families throughout Pitt County and beyond. Through partnerships with the Food Bank of Central and Eastern North Carolina, this outreach has become a consistent source of nourishment and hope for families in need. Meanwhile, The Little Queen Esther Program offers mentorship and guidance to disadvantaged young girls, instilling confidence and leadership skills that prepare them to thrive regardless of their circumstances.

Sylvia Gardner also leads the *I AM HER* Women's Empowerment Movement, an initiative that helps women reclaim their strength, identity, and purpose. Through empowerment sessions, workshops, and mentorship, she has inspired women from diverse backgrounds to lead in their homes, communities, and professional spheres.

In addition to her ministry and nonprofit work, Sylvia is the visionary behind the Born to Blossom™ clothing line—a faith-based brand created to inspire women and girls to embrace personal growth, inner beauty, and resilience through every season of life.

Sylvia holds Bachelor's degrees in both Business and Theology. She is a certified Cosmetology Instructor with the North Carolina State Board. Her diverse career reflects her commitment to excellence, faith, and service. An intercessor at heart, she discovered her calling at the age of 21 and has been faithfully walking in it ever since—serving others through prayer, worship, and the Word of God.

As an author, Sylvia Gardner brings powerful messages of hope, healing, and restoration to the page. Her writing reflects her belief that this is a divine season of restoration for women—one where their voices will be heard, their dreams revived, and their spiritual babies will leap again.

Made in United States
Orlando, FL
11 July 2025

62753916R00134